SHIRLEY

*To Judith—
Good reading
Shirley Moran*

A *River* JOURNEY, *Deep and Dear*

outskirts
press

Outskirts Press, Inc.
http://www.outskirtspress.com

ISBN: 978-1-9772-4293-8

Cover Photo © 2021 Shirley D. Meier. All rights reserved - used with permission.

Outskirts Press and the "OP" logo are trademarks belonging to Outskirts Press, Inc.

PRINTED IN THE UNITED STATES OF AMERICA

CONTENTS

Chicago 1

Amsterdam 17

Dusseldorf 33

Cologne (*Koln*) 46

Bonn 58

Koblenz 72

Heidelberg 85

Bamberg 97

Nuremberg 110

Passau 124

Vienna 136

Budapest 148

CHICAGO

THE JOURNEY STARTED out simply enough for Peter Hartman. He was retiring from Hawkins College where he had been the foreign language chairmen and everyone said that a glorious trip was the way to end thirty-five years in education and ease oneself into retirement. Even his wife, Margie, had suggested such a venture months ago.

"I've found the perfect holiday," she said as she waved a travel brochure in the air. "Let's go to Europe this time just to relax. Not to study or escort a bunch of students around."

"What, no running from house to house, eating *torte* and more *torte*? You're joking." He chuckled, thinking of the dilemma he and others had in sorting out their time and appetites when they returned to visit family and friends in their homelands.

"Look. How about a boat trip?" she said, paging though the ad. "See, they offer trips from Amsterdam to Budapest, down the Rhine, the canals and then the Danube. The Grand Tour. Sound good, doesn't it?"

"It sounds good. And expensive."

"I don't suppose we'd be able to see your sisters."

"No, not with a cruise. They live too far away in Hamburg."

"We could bill it as a retirement present. I've only got a

year more of teaching myself, you know."

"Let's think it over…," he said slowly.

Knowing that phrase was his usual turn off, she added, "Of course, if you don't want to, we could do something else."

"Sorry, it really does sound like a great idea," he said, and added in an abstract tone, "It's been a long time since I've been to Budapest, not that I saw much of it the last time."

"That's a good point. You could redo the trip to Hungary that you took as a kid during the war."

"We weren't taking a trip. We were being shipped out. Redoing that wouldn't be called a luxury cruise, I'm afraid. We slept on the hard floor and ate our meager rations out of our backpacks," he said, remembering the darkness of war time.

"Well, call it revisiting, reminiscing, perhaps reconciling. It would be good for you. Besides, I would love to see it too and I wouldn't get sea sick on the river."

So, they arranged the trip, sending in an advance payment. However, all the careful planning fell into disarray when more serious events took place.

First, there was daughter Susan and her marital trouble. It had developed slowly from trial separation at Thanksgiving that grew into a divorce before Easter. Taking eleven-year-old Mike, her only child, she moved back home in April. While struggling with the changes, they needed to settle in. Mike started at a new school even though they fully intended to get an apartment as soon as things stabilized. She found a job but her position required a special month-long training session in the summer.

Just as that situation became clear, Margie's mother, Bea, fell and broke her hip. She managed the replacement surgery well enough for someone eighty-five years old, but her rehabiliation was slow going and she needed extra help after her dismissal. Margie couldn't run daily trips to her mother's home in Wisconsin, so there was nothing to do but bring her back to their house in suburban Chicago.

"What a glorious opportunity to clean out the study," said Margie without a lot of enthusiasm. "But we needed to do this anyway."

Reshuffling was necessary as Grandmother Bea would need to occupy the first-floor room they used as a library and office. Their refined collection of books and papers ended up going to one corner of the recreation room in the basement whose ping pong table had already been replaced by a bed and desk for Mike. Susan occupied the guest room, which was actually her former bedroom. Their other daughter, Tracy, would soon come home from college for a summer job so she'd be back in her old bedroom too, the last free space remaining.

"Four generations under one roof. A full house, they say in cards," said Margie.

"Looks more like a grand slam to me," said Peter dryly.

"It shouldn't be for too long. I'm sure we can manage. Tracy will be working so she'll not be around much and Susan will be gone for part of the time. Hopefully Mother will be able to go back home soon."

"Ha, get real, Margie. She can't stay by herself anymore. You know that. We'll have to face the fact." Only last night they had found her on the edge of her wet bed, her walker pushed aside. She was totally unaware of the time or that she had ripped her nightgown. Yes, specialized care was probably going to be needed in the near future.

"Then there's Mike. What's he supposed to do?" Peter wondered.

"What all eleven-year-old boys do, I expect."

"Which is?"

"You should know. You've been one, my dear. You can concentrate on him while I help Mother."

"A great start for us on our special retirement. Freedom to do your thing, they say," Peter moaned.

"There goes our trip too, I suppose," Margie added. She hugged him for a long moment. "But it's the thing to do."

"Of course, it's the right thing and the only thing to do," he answered, looking into her eyes with tenderness. She was the one who would be pulled the hardest, he knew.

However, a few days later Margie added a different perspective when she saw Mike sprint directly down to his room. "He's like a rabbit, dashing to his hole. I followed him and saw him clamp on his head set and sprawl on the bed."

"So, what did you say?"

"I told him I'd like to talk. But he couldn't hear me with those things on so I had to wave my hands until he pulled them off."

"So, what did he say?"

"What's up, Grandma?"

"And you stammered, right?"

"Exactly. I'm always flustered but he said he was OK and wondered why I asked. But Pete, he didn't smile. He never smiles, just answers in one-liners. Susan says all kids of his age are like that now days but I don't think his mother is able to see things clearly. Not her fault exactly, with the divorce and all the turmoil, but that boy needs a different focus."

"Yes, he seems lonely, distant sometimes. As I remember, the girls were never like that. They were the opposite, especially as teenagers. Usually screaming about something or other. But Mike, poor kid, we've got to expect some of that after a divorce. I suppose."

Margie nodded her head in agreement. "He didn't have much of a chance to get settled into the new school here before the end of the year. He spent time doodling with his art project, sometimes writing in his journal for English but no real connection."

It was indeed a trying time for them all. He knew the nights of interrupted sleep tending to her mother were taking a toll on Margie. Peaking in the study bedroom, he saw that Bea was now asleep, looking peaceful and refreshed, but another fall was in the making and her confusion increasing. The time for assistance from the Medicare aid, who came two days a week, would soon run out. Thank goodness the school year was almost over.

"We've got to call and cancel the trip," said Peter at breakfast.

"Before you do that, I think I have a better idea. You should take Mike with you on that trip. The boy needs a summer of stimulation and," she said, almost uttering out loud that Peter also needed some time to regroup. "It would be good for you both, ease up the space here a bit too."

"Leave you here? Absolutely not," he said automatically. With the exception of taking some educational courses away from home through the years, they had always traveled together. And how they'd enjoyed those many car trips with the girls and their dog, Schnitzer, he remembered with a pang.

Margie continued, "Susan and Tracy need to work and get their lives on track. And it will give me a chance to deal with Mother, sort out what we're going to do. It's a rocky time and you men will just be in the way. It's as simple as that."

"Funny, funny."

"Not funny, my dear. Just fun. Have fun, you and Mike.

You could make it a guy thing, as they say," she giggled, then added a sober note. "His father has faded from the scene and we ladies just don't reach him very well, I'm afraid."

"Oh, you've done pretty well with this damn business," said Peter, uncomfortably moving in his chair. "I don't get through to him any better than you. It just takes time."

"Time, that's it. It's the time to do this," she said. "For both of you, Pete."

So, it was decided. After a few phone calls, the arrangements were made. To rally interest, Peter showed greater excitement than he actually felt when talking about it to Mike, who remained rather passive but obliging.

On the flight, Mike had the window seat and strained toward it, looking out as they took off from O'Hare. He'd traveled on a plane before as a toddler, but this would be the first flight that he'd remember. The terminals and runways skimmed by and then the plane lifted up, passing over the industrial parks and neighborhoods of Chicago. Soon they saw Sears Tower, the Amoco and Hancock buildings, standing as sentinels with their tips pushing above the rest of the sprouting skyscrapers.

"Wow, you see that?" Mike said as the plane flew over the Loop and Lake Shore Drive, now basking in the late afternoon sunshine, before heading toward Lake Michigan. "It looks so awesome from up here."

"You're right. Impressive, isn't it?" Peter smiled at the boy's boisterous outburst. He'd heard so few actual words of delight from Mike in the past few months that it seemed very refreshing. Perhaps this trip would help him.

"Take a good look at it because we'll be seeing very different cities in Europe."

"How are they so different, Gramps?"

"Well, most are not so tall, so new, so raw, so...impatient, you could say."

"What do you mean by that?"

"Well, in Europe most buildings are older. They've got traditional curves and arches, that sort of thing. Streets are often crooked and narrow. Not like Chicago. Look, do you see the straight lines and square blocks down there?"

"Yeah, it's kind of like Grandma's quilt."

"Good comparison, Mike. She should call it the Chicago quilt." The perceptive remark made him smile.

From the air, Chicago was indeed a flat, right angle city except for some of the prominent rail and interstate road lines that stood out, slicing through the grid in different directions. Trains, cars and planes were visibly the reasons why this mid-American city became the nation's hub of transportation. Though it had both the Chicago River, colored green on St. Pat's day, and the magnificent lake, the waterways served only as secondary adornments to modern Chicago.

How different, he thought, that was in comparison to Cologne and Vienna. With so many historic points along the route, he'd have a chance to tell Mike why the river cities had been the European links to civilization and development for countless ages. The present busy commercial and tourist water traffic would show them their modern importance, too. That was the point of such a cruise, of course, and he hoped the boy would appreciate it.

As the plane turned slightly, Peter looked automatically back toward the northwest suburbs. Home and work were there, indistinct now in the fading green pattern, but there. Hawkins College, a place of so many faces, books and memories, with its circling walkways would be quiet now before the summer session. Its brick buildings, surrounded by parking lots and a lake, and his former office, now with the shades drawn and waiting for a new occupant, still seemed part of him. But he knew that it would have to fade just as the landscape below him was quickly receding into the distance.

He closed his eyes briefly. Chicago, Chicago. The familiar city of the big shoulders had been Peter's home for forty years and it had been good to him. Thinking back when he first came from Europe long ago, he could still feel the sensation of this vibrant American city. Chicago wasn't all glory and honey, of course, but it had helped him become an American. Here he had his education, work, friends and family.

He thought of his youth. Life in Germany had been tough during the war, with air raid sirens and nightly bombing. His father was gone early on. Terrible were the many times when he and his sisters were herded into the basement shelter by their mother and grandmother. Once upon coming out, they saw the neighboring building a smoldering mass. He remembered how dangerous it was a few weeks later when three men carefully pulled out an unexploded bomb which had slid through the coal chute into the basement of their own apartment house.

The aftermath for them following the war was actually harder, even when machines started to plow away the debris in the streets. Many buildings were destroyed and the damaged remainders were like honey combs after a bear's raid, with gapping holes and exposed interiors. There was the quiet hunger of little food available, making do with clothing too small, even the embarrassment of needing to wear his grandmother's shoes.

During quiet nights he and his older buddy Klaus would climb the fence at the occupying English army supply depot, making sure that their buckets didn't clang. Stealing coal briquettes appealed to their young sense of adventure, but the silent look of relief on his mother's face when he returned with his filled bucket gave him pride. It was the only source of heat they had. Providing for the family came early.

Money was meager for his mother and grandmother and the goods available to buy, even more so. Bartering was common but they had little to barter. Schools were still closed and there was almost no access to books and learning. He needed to work and fortunately found a job at a relief center. It brought in a few helpful marks but ended his formal German education. Later in America, he took competency tests, fudged on his missing proof of secondary education and was admitted as a foreign student. He was allowed to continue to study, something he would not have been able to do in Germany.

He now remembered that one breakthrough event of the war that inspired the trip to Hungary. Because of the damage and closed schools, organized efforts called the *Kinderlandverschickung* were made to send children away for safe keeping. He'd been sent to Hungary for six months to escape the bombing danger. Many older ones, like his sister Marie, had already gone to work situations in small towns and his other sister, Anna, was sent to go to the country with an aunt in the Sauerland. But there was some debate over what to do with him.

Peter was still too young to enter military service in '43 and his widowed mother, struggling with the strain of the bombing, knew he would be safe away from Dusseldorf. But his grandmother, now living with them because her apartment had been destroyed, didn't want Peter away from her guidance and the church. In the end, however, they reluctantly allowed him to join a boys' troupe being sent to Hungary. They would stay with ethnic Germans along with supervisors and teachers provided for them by the government. Being scared and confused, he begged to stay home even if his friend Klaus was also going. But the bombs overhead determined the answer.

He was eleven, like Mike, that summer when he departed on his journey to Hungary which took him down the Rhine and onto a train to Passau, where they boarded another boat on the Danube for Budapest. There they were divided into groups of about thirty boys each and picked up by ethnic German host families, most of whom lived in a rural area south of the Hungarian capital.

Their camp, consisting of sleeping tents, supply sheds and some roofed shelters, was set up on the property but they ate with the families. For Peter, coming from a household of women, the company of boys his own age and living in the country, away from cities at war and shortages, was something new. His anxiety was lessened when he discovered that the routine chores weren't hard, and the time for lessons was shortened. They didn't have church attendance and a comfortable atmosphere surrounded them. He found himself relaxing and the change was suddenly appealing. This first taste of adventure and some independence was a wonderful experience for him but after six months with the cold weather coming, they had to return home. The war was still going on.

His thoughts returned to his present family and he saw their split-level house on Beaver Street with its brown cedar siding and white shutters. This morning his favorite pink and white peonies were in abundant bloom against the side of the garage. The short honeysuckle hedge displayed a tinge of rosy blossoms and the vibrant lawn, which he and Mike cut the night before, swirled around his wife's flower garden

Their house in the suburbs could have been the poster

ad for the realization of the conventional American dream, he mused. It was a comfortable place, not as grand as some of the newer neighbors, but never the less a solid residence that had taken them years to mold. They'd made the office addition, a utility shed and a play yard which used to have an above ground swimming pool when the girls were young.

And Margie had planted trees, far too many trees. A few had died but most were still alive and beautiful, in spite of the fact that she had often moved them from one spot to another. Yes, his wife, the farmer's daughter, hadn't yet realized her final goal of the perfect garden, but she had succeeded in instilling in him, the city boy, a pride in his acre plot of nature.

About now she and Susan should be returning home from the airport, pulling into the newly paved driveway. Glancing up to see the planes high overhead, coming and going to one of the world's busiest airport, she'd throw a kiss at the sky and hear her daughter's soft voice beside her say, "Gee, Mom, that's sweet. Let's hope they'll be all right."

"Oh, don't worry. We're all in God's hands, one way or another." She'd smile, not with her natural exuberance but with controlled assurance, knowing the present required a positive upper lip. He could hear her say to Susan, "Now let's go see how Tracy has fared with your grandmother."

The broad southern curve of the lake became visible through the plane's window and Peter looked toward Indiana. Over that horizon lay Mike's previous home and he wondered if the boy might also turn to look but his grandson continued to stare at the lake below them, interested in the numerous boats which were just miniature dots jutting about in the midst of the sparkling glints of light caught on the waves. Probably he wasn't oriented to the right direction or didn't care to revisit Indiana at the moment.

Perhaps when they got back, he'd take Mike sailing. Another one of those guy things, as Margie might say. Having grown up in a household of women and then producing another one on his own, Peter appreciated his grandson. He'd have to find more things to keep the boy interested, that's for sure. Cutting the grass with the riding mower had proved popular and with a little practice, the boy would get the hang of it.

Actually, he showed some natural technique, not like the girls. Peter remembered their first weaving efforts on the tractor, barely missing the fence, clipping several trees and almost running into the creek. Their introduction to power movement included the tricky obstacle course of deadly rose and barberry bushes, as well as their dog running interference. Possibly that practice made them the safe automobile drivers they were as adults.

However, Tracy, howling with laughter, told a very different version of the story recently. "Oh, Dad, you should have seen yourself. Running after us and yelling, waving your arms. Over there, no, over here. For God's sake, watch where you're going!"

Susan piped in. "You forgot his smoky language, Sister. Lots of swearing, mostly in German. I think the whole neighborhood waited for our Saturday morning sessions. It certainly gave them a colorful diversion from the quiet boredom of the week."

"Now, now, girls, it wasn't that bad," interrupted Margie, knowing Peter was a bit touchy about the subject. She viewed her husband as a mild-mannered man who seldom lost his temper but when it happened, she was a good referee.

Chicago was behind them now as the plane climbed up among light clouds. Lost to them were the haunts of his early days in America but the bulging buildings of Midwest Printing still stood on the west side, he knew. They were the successful creation of his older distant cousins, the men who had sponsored him as an immigrant. He'd worked there on and off for years, grateful for the salary, not generous by American standards, but considered appropriate for an immigrant family member. He had been expected to stay there indefinitely but his widening American experience and eagerness for an education had changed that.

Family and work had consumed his years. He had closed his mind to his former life, not wanting to remember that time. He seldom spoke of growing up and never expressed his view about the war years. Margie respected that, knowing some part of him was sensitive about his past. She knew he just wanted to fit into modern America and he had succeeded. Her recent suggestion about the trip did subtly suggest, however, an opening to his European past.

He easily traced his early memories in Illinois, remembering the University of Illinois campus where he met Margie, the commute on the EL, their first apartment in the converted farmhouse when Susan had been a baby. Then came Tracy with an early delivery at the fire station because Margie fell down, bringing on quick labor, right in front of the place. And there was the tornado that damaged most of the roof of their new house but mercifully nothing else. No more children came, but Snitzer, a grey Schnauzer, entered their lives one Christmas Eve and stayed around for 14 years.

The Chagall windows at the Art Institute, the Egyptian mummies at the Field Museum, and the fish at the aquarium were all part of their typical mid-western Chicago education. The girls played in the high school band during the Bears' half time at Soldier's Field. They liked seeing the German U Boat and the coal mine at the Science and Industry Museum, interesting and ironic facts given that he was from near the Ruhr, the industrial German heartland famous for coal and steel.

Looking at the holiday windows on State Street, before the malls invaded their life, was a ritual, as well as eating lunch at the Berghof Restaurant. Once later when Susan came home with Mike as a baby, he'd been so noisy and restless at the restaurant that they'd rolled him, stroller and all, right under the table out of view. He promptly went to sleep, quite unaware of the clatter and chatter around him. Meanwhile they quickly ate their sauerbraten and red cabbage before the male waiters scooped their plates up and away. Food and efficiency were a great Teutonic tradition in Chicago and in most places where Germans lived, he thought.

Mike asked Peter to get his carryon bag from the luggage rack. The boy opened it, searching for something, probably the action figures he'd packed. Suddenly his hand pulled out a small portfolio containing note pad, letter paper and envelopes. A note from Margie was pasted on top. It said, "Mike, draw some pictures about places you see and send us some cards so we can be part of your trip too. Have a wonderful time! Love, Gramsy."

A huge smile covered the boy's face. He rummaged into the bag again and pulled out a small carton of colored pencils. "Grandpa, you see these?"

"Sure do. Your grandmother likes surprises, just like you, I guess."

Yes, it might be just the thing for Mike, a quiet and withdrawn spirit needing an outlet, Peter thought as the boy flipped open the cover and enthusiastically started to sketch.

Peter suspected that Margie probably counted on the activity to help them both get through some awkward times on the trip. Quickly, tall straight buildings appeared beside a wavy sea on the tablet page and he scribbled "Chicago" on the top. Not too bad, thought Peter.

The aircraft traveled across Michigan and into forested Canada. Mike watched the video screen showing the route and poked his grandfather every time the line moved farther along the tract. Halfway across the Atlantic, after the meal and a movie, Mike fell asleep but Peter couldn't relax. He'd read the in-flight magazine and scanned the Tribune highlights about the war in Yugoslavia; but of course, it wasn't Yugoslavia any more. Shifting borders in that part of the world had been a problem for centuries. His part of Hungary had become part of Yugoslavia after the war; now there was Bosnia, Serbia, Croatia and whatever else. Rummaging through his case for his spy thriller, he read a few pages but put it away when the lights dimmed.

Looking at his grandson curled awkwardly in the belted seat beside him, he inspected the tow-headed boy. He was a cute kid who resembled Susan a great deal with fair skin, straight and thick hair around his still childish face. Though slender in the body, his feet and hands were large, forecasting a tall frame like his father.

"Oh, how'd they talk me into this?" Peter muttered.

Susan had heartily endorsed the generous offer of the trip for Mike, saying it was just the thing for him. She mentioned how much she valued the family excursions they'd had through the years but she wept as she clutched her son at the gate. Her eyes had been such a well of anguish that Peter had to look away.

"We're flying away, going to see places on this journey,

my boy." But what are we trying to discover? And what are we going to find? he whispered to himself.

Mike, lost deep in his sleep, didn't ask any questions but Peter struggled with the answers to his own questions.

AMSTERDAM

AFTER LANDING AT Schiphol Airport in the morning and getting through customs, Peter emerged with Mike into the crowded lobby where uniformed travel guides waved banners and signs.

"Hey, if that isn't luck," he said, pointing to a tall woman wearing glasses and dressed in a blue suit with tote bag and backpack. "Our tour leader is right up front."

Her sign said World Wonder Tours in bright gold letters but her name plate simply read Emma. He immediately saw their names, Peter Hartman and Michael Johnson, listed among several others on the sign.

They scrambled to join her and Peter heard a slight accent, educated and smooth, as she greeted them. Her smile was welcoming as she said, "I'm to be your guide for the entire trip. We'll be on our way just as soon as we find the others." She handed out name tags for them from her tote bag and he heard Mike mutter that it seemed like they were going on a field trip in school. Quickly she rounded up the rest and they were on their way to a van which took them out of the airport into the city.

All the passengers looked like they were Americans - an older couple, a single man and a skinny red headed girl about Mike's age who was in company of a smart looking older woman, perhaps the grandmother, wearing a colorful scarf. Peter was glad there was someone the boy's age as he presumed the majority of the tourists would be retired people. He saw the youngsters exchange glances, but Mike immediately looked down when he saw the girl's eyes lighten, her smile revealing a big set of shinning braces.

"Mike, here's your first taste of Europe," Peter said, looking around as they left the building and headed for the waiting van.

"Well, then, where's the food?" Mike responded, obviously trying to be funny. Likely he was hungry, even if they had just eaten breakfast before landing.

"Don't worry. You'll get good chow here. They usually top everything with real whipped cream."

"Where are we going now?"

"To the boat, The Majestic. Our floating hotel, you could say. It will be nice. Just settle in for the trip. No banging around on the train or finding a room, packing and unpacking. That's something your grandmother would have really liked. We have a city tour this afternoon."

The van pulled up to a dock next to a long sleek triple decked river boat, gleaming white in the water with blue horizontal stripes that ran along the water's edge and the roof lines of the decks. He'd taken the family out on a Lake Michigan cruise once but that boat had been considerably smaller than this one.

"Gee, lots of flags," said Mike noticing the array that was flying from the mast. "It looks like a carnival."

"More like a car dealer's lot," joked Peter. "Actually, they represent some of the countries that we'll be seeing."

A steward, welcoming them to the Majesty, led them to

their cabin, which was located on the upper deck. The porter who brought in their luggage also welcomed them and beamed at the tip Peter offered. After they left, the two travelers looked around. The pleasant room was wood paneled with a sliding glass door which opened to a small balcony. It had twin beds, dresser, desk, an ample closet, TV and telephone.

"Well, we paid for a top accommodation and I think we got it," said Peter. "Check out the bathroom." Peter knew he liked to take long showers.

"It's not as big as the one at the Holiday Inn," said Mike. "But they got a hair dryer and lots of soap and towels."

"Well, it's big enough and we won't spend too much time in there anyway. You'll need a different mindset around here, Mike. Things are condensed on a boat. That also goes along with being in Europe, especially Holland. Did you know that Amsterdam is one of the most crowded cities in the world, people per square inch?"

Mike moved to the balcony door, sliding it open for a better view. Gulls flew over and around the boat, creating a peppered sky of white blurs and sound. Outside they could see the river full of water craft, not only cruise ships anchored tightly together along the banks but houseboats, barges and small motorboats moving about.

"Gee, where are they all going?" Mike asked his grandfather.

"Everywhere. Lot of hauling is done on the rivers and at sea. We'll be going up the Rhine from here, then the Main and the connecting canals to the Danube."

"I like that one," the boy said, pointing to a large green houseboat with white trim that was coming by. He grabbed his sketch pad and started outlining the boat.

Scores of barrels and crates were stacked on the top deck,

in addition to several bicycles and a motorcycle. A TV dish was attached to the cabin as well as some other antennas. There were crisp lace curtains at the windows, pots full of flowers, even a strung clothes line with wash and lanterns hanging from it. Several spotted cats lay on the crates and a dog looked over the side as though he were inspecting the bumper tires strapped to the boat. A burly man, smoking a pipe, was walking on deck and they heard laughter coming from below.

"That's a family home and a business, all in one," said Peter.

"Looks like it could be fun."

"But lots of work too. We've got a better deal here, believe me."

After unpacking, they went to a nearby bank and exchanged money. He showed the strange bills to Mike. "We won't need much here, just enough to get a few things now and then. The city tours are included as well as breakfast and dinner."

"Do we eat on board ship?" Mike asked, eyeing a street stand.

"Usually, according to the brochure. Sometimes we're to have a special dinner at a local restaurant. But we've got time before the tour bus gets here and it's almost noon. I bet you're hungry. How about the place over there?"

They stepped gingerly around metal containers filled with flowers for sale that surrounded the stand. Then they looked at the food offerings.

"No hamburgers or French fries?" Mike looked at his grandfather.

"Doesn't look like it. But they've got good rolls and look at that cheese." His own appetite kicked in as he looked at the crisp bread but Mike frowned. "You'll have to get used to different food. Different names too. Take hamburger, for instance. If you order that here, you might get a ham sandwich. We supposedly adapted the bun and beef combo from the folks in Hamburg, using the name, not the ingredients. Same goes for French fries. And if you order a *weiner schnitzal*, you won't get any kind of weiner or hot dog either."

"Oh, I know that from your house when Grandma made it. She told me it was a special dish from Vienna but I still don't know why they call it *weiner schnitzel*."

"Vienna is actually *"Wein"* in German. A cutlet that's made in the *Wein* style is called *weiner schnitzel* in Austria. But actually, that isn't Austria either, the country is *Oestreich* in German." Peter heard himself talking in his teacher mode and saw that Mike was losing interest in the semantics. No need to overwhelm him, for the complexity of language would soon become apparent enough as they went on, he knew.

"Let's order a cheese sandwich and pop. OK? They've got that."

Mike crunched away on the hard and crispy bread and seemed to find it satisfying. The growing boy's surging appetite might serve him well in the cuisine discovery department. He well remembered his daughters' reluctance years ago when they first encountered continental cooking and how they changed their minds.

People and bicycles swirled around them on the narrow street running alongside the river. The tiny clinging of the bicycle bells competed with the car horns and the occasional boat blast. They didn't get to wander any further because three busses pulled up and people coming from the Majestic started to board. It looked like the passenger count would have to be well over a hundred. Emma and the other travel guides were each standing by the door of a bus so they headed toward hers.

"Hello, hello everyone doing our first city tour here in Amsterdam. I always carry this blue umbrella, closed at the moment, so you can always find me", she said waving it high above her. She then passed out a city map from her tote bag for the travelers to follow.

Peter liked the cheerful sound of her voice. It had a friendly lilt to it and she smiled at them, clearly recognizing them. She even winked at Mike. Suddenly he saw the resemblance to his sister Anna when she was young, with very similar coloring and features. Yes, Anna was always somewhere in his mind.

Seated at the front, Emma turned on her mike and announced the route they'd take. "Amsterdam is one of the largest historical centers in the world," she said. "First we're going to see the Royal Palace which also has served as the town hall. It's located in the city center called the Dam."

"That's a mighty strange name," said his grandson. "But it must have something to do with all the water and dikes and stuff like that, right."

"Right," said Peter but he thought, the kid's taking an interest.

As they drove, she started a historical summary of the Netherlands but Peter saw Mike's eyes soon wander, preferring to look at the little cars and bicyclists weaving around the bus. An older woman who looked Asian, her skirt flying around her legs on the bike, expertly hung on to the bus for free locomotion and looking up, smiled at him as he peered down at her. The bus turned, and in a moment, she was gone in another direction.

"Lots of Hollanders are from southeast Asia. The Dutch

had colonies all over the world and many came here to live," Peter explained. "Now they have many people from all over, especially Eastern Europe, the Balkans."

They wound their way along crowded canals and streets where gabled buildings stood side by side, their multi-colored brick facades of beige, gray and cinnamon shining in the sun. They were usually three or four stories high, narrow and long, with tiled roofs. Some had only a door and single window on the ground floor, with the gable end serving as the front of the house. The peaked roof line rose in steps to the top.

"Their buildings are sure pretty odd looking," said Mike, tracing their lines in his sketchbook.

"You know in wild west movies they had false fronts, sort of like these."

"People live here?"

"Yes, usually above the shop that's on the first floor."

"Did you live above a store when you were a kid?"

"Yes, in an apartment. That's how most Europeans lived. They still don't have as many suburbs with private homes like we do in America."

The brick row houses wrapping around the network of tiny streets facing the canals seemed like an endless maze. Mike looked up and noticed the top of the buildings. Each one had a different emblem on it, most of them carved in stone. Some looked like a coat of arms and others depicted sailing ships or animals.

"Must be a rich guy," Mike said, noting a special front of red brick that had lots of niches with carved figures standing in them. Flipping the pages, he sketched quick new house fronts with circular patterns in imitation of the carvings on the doors. On the roofs he drew a small coat of arms and a sail boat.

"Probably was," said Peter, noting Mike's observations and reproductions.

"That house says fifteen eighty-two and the next one is sixteen-forty. Seems a funny way to have house numbers." Mike added small numbers to his houses.

"It tells when the house was built. The Roman numerals say the same thing."

Almost all of the houses had large beams with pulleys extending out from the top of the gables. Peter told him they were used to haul up furniture and supplies. The stairs and hallways were usually too narrow to maneuver anything large. In fact, often the passageways allowed only enough room for a single person at a time to navigate.

"They have those beams on barns in Indiana," said Mike. "You know, my father had friends that lived in the country and we used to go visit them. Had lots of hay fights in the loft with the kids. We'd swing out from that beam on the rope. That is, until we got yelled at."

"That's pretty dangerous all right, but I remember doing something like that too when I was a kid. In Hungary, out in the country."

"Yeah, really?" He shook his head, somewhat in disbelief. "That's cool."

Then came the Dam and the big square with the palace ahead of them. It was a solid straight building with rows of windows on the side and a big round tower on top. Emma was talking about the first houses in Amsterdam being built in the 11th century and the city becoming the capital in the 1600's.

"She's got that right," Mike said. "Everything looks mighty old, even ancient."

A mixed group of people, several with made up faces,

were performing some sort of play or game on the sidewalk. A horse with an elaborate harness and bells went by, pulling an equally decorated tourist carriage with driver and two Japanese passengers. The horse puffed and snorted, the driver whistled and snapped the whip but it didn't hit the animal. The bicycles, tooting and clanging, also whizzed around them, but neither horse nor man, knowing their own superiority, paid attention to them. The snorting and snapping were repeated, most likely a staged sound effect for the benefit of the paying audience in the rear seats.

They drove by the Central Train Station where the area in front was totally filled with a crunch of people. To the side, travelers, pulling suitcases or hauling backpacks, walked in and around the many young people who were sitting or lying about. Some were stretched out asleep and most of them looked pretty scruffy. Some of the people in the bus whispered and muttered, looking at the scene.

"We're tolerant of the world's youth that come here but it does make for a mass of humanity in one spot, doesn't it?" Emma explained tactfully.

"I bet she won't tell us about the drug scene or their famous red-light district," said the lady behind them to her companion.

Emma continued smoothly, "This metropolis is a study in contrasts, from the sublime to the offbeat. You'll be passing by universities and hospitals, places of business and the harbor, all within a short distance of one another, and the famous red-light district."

Peter heard the lady cough. He smiled but looked straight ahead, avoiding Mike's eyes. As they drove around a corner, a series of open narrow windows on the upper floors displayed what appeared to be painted mannequins, all wearing jewelry and shining dresses. They could almost be store displays, he thought, except they were moving, beckoning to the passing crowd. Big signs on the street said SEX and Mike scrunched down in his seat uncomfortable but Peter saw his eyes rivet back to the windows as they turned the corner. He didn't offer an explanation.

"We'll be following the series of canals that define this city," said Emma after a bit. "You'll soon see why there are more than eight hundred bridges in Amsterdam."

The bus slowed because of the traffic and a man with a monkey strapped to his leg was playing a hurdy-gurdy barrel organ right next to the window. A pitch man came by selling watches and wallets while two very skilled skate boarders darted in and among the crowd. Mike watched their moves, nodding his head in approval.

And people were everywhere. The flow of bicycles continued around them as Emma went on with her history lesson. After six or seven more bridges and canals, Peter saw Mike nod off, his head hitting his chest. He immediately straightened up and wiped his brow, glancing at his grandfather, but soon he was slumping and dozing again.

Mike missed the *Montelban* Tower, once part of the defensive wall of the city, and the Mint Tower, where they used to make money. The boy's eyes fluttered open a bit as they passed along the harbor called the Y which was once part of the *Zyder Zee* but then he was asleep again. Peter nodded a few times also. The sun and sway of the boat along with jet lag were getting to Peter too because he felt very weary himself.

One side of the harbor had sea-going vessels in dry dock where cranes and scaffolds filled the sky and equipment and carts filled the docks beside them. A glass topped tourist boat, low in the water, appeared beside a tug which had a big orange butterfly design on the bow. Peter thought the boy would like that one but didn't disturb him until Emma's voice rang out, helping to waken him. "And now we have the *Magere Brug*, or the Slender Bridge, over the Amstel River. It's the most famous drawbridge in Amsterdam and a good spot for your tour to end today. The Majestic is waiting for you right down the street. Have a good dinner and tomorrow morning, I'll meet you again for a few hours in our museum district."

"So, what did you think?" Peter asked his grandson as they left the bus.

Mike rubbed his eyes. "It was pretty good, Grandpa. But did she say dinner?"

"Yes, yes. You catch the important stuff."

And a fine dinner it was. The tour company provided a splendid buffet, filled with lots of cheese dishes. Everyone wore a name tag and a big globe in the center of the table had pins with little flags stuck in it to point out all the passenger's hometowns. Lots of Americans, many retired or soon to be, were in the majority with a smattering of Europeans and Asians of various ages. A teenage choral group from Norway was on board and they provided various musical selections.

Mike saw the young redheaded girl nearby but was ready to turn away when her companion skillfully involved them in a little get-acquainted conversation. She said she was Julie Upshaw, originally from Buffalo, New York, but called London her home now. "I got the job to show her the world while her mother was off on her honeymoon. Lucky because I was going on this cruise anyway."

"Just like Auntie Mame, I suppose," said Peter.

"I'd like to think so," said Julie. "But I'm not half so witty. My specialty is travel but I've got a big thing about art too."

"Those are my interests also. This cruise will be a good

time for you."

"And me too," said the girl smiling and revealing her braces. "My specialty is castles and robber barons."

Peter laughed. "And you are?"

"Talented, tormented and terrible at spelling."

"No, I mean your name."

"Oh, excuse me," said Julie. "This is Karen Higgins, my
niece. Kari for short." She added with a laugh, "but Carrot for
fun."

Mike looked at the girl, expecting some normal outrage at
the remark, even if she did indeed have flaming copper hair.
But Karen or Kari or Carrot wasn't tormented at all. She looked
positively pleased. He was wondering what would actually
bother this precocious girl when his grandfather interrupted.
"This is Michael, my grandson, also along to see the world. I
don't know too much about his spelling but he is pretty sharp
with the pencil when it comes to drawing."

Mike squirmed a bit at that disclosure but they were soon
swept along to their table. Peter was watching him and smiling, thinking about the boy's shyness and great appetite. His
lean growing body didn't show any harmful effect of overin-
dulgence but Peter touched his own slightly bulging stomach.
That's one blessing of being young, he thought as he resisted
a second piece of cake.

The next morning, after a satisfying breakfast of scrambled
eggs, cheese and hard rolls called *brotchen* for Mike, they
were off in the tour bus again with bubbling Emma, dressed
totally in green today but with the same blue umbrella as their
flag.

"Good morning, group. Are you ready to see more of
Amsterdam? Yes? Good, good. It's the only city in the world
where the most famous people are artists. Yes, that's right.

Rembrandt is more famous here, and in the world, than any of our rulers. And we can't forget to mention other significant artists that are featured in the Rijksmuseum like Vermeer and Van Dyke. We'll also be going to see the special museum featuring Van Gogh's work. He's easily the favorite artist that Holland has ever produced. Now his paintings are priceless but in his life time he couldn't sell a thing."

"Also, today we shall go to the Anne Frank house and see where she and her family actually lived during part of World War II. This is where she wrote her famous diary, now translated into many languages from around the world. It describes her family's life in hiding during the Nazi occupation in Amsterdam. It's considered an amazing testament for such a young girl."

Peter looked at Mike. He seemed to be paying attention. It should be a good day for him as his love of sketching could probably sustain his interest in the museums and Anne Frank might appeal to him too, being a girl his own age when the war came.

"Have you ever read that book, the Diary of Anne Frank?" asked Peter.

Mike smiled slightly, perhaps in embarrassment. "Nope, but I've heard of it, I think."

"That's all right. You'll probably get it next year in school. It's a staple in junior high. She was just about your age, writing down her daily thoughts, sort of what you like to do with your drawing."

"Oh, yeah?"

"She became famous for her writing but never in her lifetime."

"Why, what happened to her?"

"She died in the war." Somehow, he couldn't elaborate

so he said, "they'll tell you all about that when we go there."

They passed an historic windmill. Emma instructed, "Look at that national symbol of Holland, built in 1636. It's special because there aren't many of the old ones around anymore, certainly not in the city, but if you went into the country, you'd have a better chance to see one. We still use wind as a power source, however, as the Low Countries do not have turbulent water sources. You probably will recognize the modern windmills on the landscape because they have big blades that look like airplane propellers."

They arrived at the grand old dame of a building complete with twin towers that housed the Rijks Museum. A wealth of visual treasures awaited them, but much of the commentary was lost on Mike, as well as some of the other older group members. The boy did stand entranced before Rembrandt's Night Watch. When they moved to the modern Van Gogh museum, things picked up. The space and light of the building and the color of the paintings created a special appeal, even if most of them were small and a great crunch of people was in the galleries.

Pete found it a wonderful experience but didn't press for any oral reaction from Mike because he knew that many more museums were on the itinerary and he didn't want overload. Mike said his favorite was the early dark moody painting of Van Gogh's named "Potato Eaters". Apparently, the strong black and white tones appealed to him as he copied it in pencil.

After a quick lunch they were off to the Anne Frank house. Another very crowded situation greeted them. Emma gave them a brief introduction but the first floor which housed a holocaust museum was very crowded and for time and comfort, they went to the second story where they could see the actual rooms that the family had lived in during the war. At that time, the entrance was hidden behind a large bookcase, and even now with the rooms empty of furniture, they appeared small. Anne's bedroom held the most interest for both of them.

"Look at that," said Mike, pointing to the wall, now safely covered with glass but showing some of Anne's magazine pin ups and writings. She had favorite stars or heroes, just like kids his own age. A bronze bust of Anne stood quietly by the window. Outside a flock of pigeons flapped about and rose up into the sky. Church bells rang in the distance, just as they had when a young girl looked to the sky there and wrote the lines, "that in spite of all that happened, people were generally good". Margie had that same persuasion but Peter knew his own cynic nature sometimes impeded such a basic belief.

"People are quiet in here, aren't they?" whispered Mike.

"Yes. It's a special place, kind of like a church or synagogue." He sighed. Let this be Mike's strongest impression. We can talk more about this later because the boy didn't need to be terrorized or drowned with the holocaust at this point.

So then why I am taking this trip to yesteryear with Mike? he questioned himself again. Justification surfaced immediately. Of course, he wanted his young grandson to see to world, good and bad, today and yesterday, with eyes open. He'd experienced severe hardships too but even today he could not express them as clearly as Anne had in her diary with her childlike optimism.

Peter swallowed hard and went on. "You know she was rather like Van Gogh in a way, people with hidden talents who really had to struggle in lonely circumstances. I think their search for expression helped them a lot." He was also thinking of Mike.

"That could be, Grandpa."

When they returned to the boat, they had a sit-down meal with arranged places. Julie and Kari, really dressed up, were seated at the next table. After they turned in, the boat started out of the city, with the illuminated towers and glittering city lights surrounding them. The lighted bridges were especially interesting because their sparkling reflections, depending on the construction, formed mirrored circles or squares in the water.

"Well, we're off to Dusseldorf, Mike. Be there in the morning."

"That's good," replied the sleepy boy. "I want to see your hometown"

"We'll leave the tour group for the entire day there to visit my cousins, Emil and Johan. All that's left there after my mother died. My sisters both moved to Hamburg years ago. No museums but I'll show you around. It will be fun seeing them again."

"Do they have kids?"

"Johann never married and lived with his mother all his life. She died just a few years ago. Emil had family but I'm afraid they're grown up. They have grandkids but I'm not sure where they all live now," replied Peter with a yawn.

He saw his grandson's eyes close and he too was soon asleep. The softly swaying boat traveled through the Dutch countryside, passing quiet places that had seen two noisy hard wars. Neither of them knew when they entered Germany (*Deutschland*) during the night.

DUSSELDORF

AS PROMISED, COUSINS Johann and Emil, accompanied by his wife Helga, were at dockside the next morning. They were both slender tall men with thinning blonde hair, fading blue eyes and ruddy complexions. Standing between them, Helga was a study in contrasts as she was short, dark and heavier. She was groomed with the latest hair style and all were dressed in casual but expensive sport clothes. Helga had gold jewelry chains and bracelets dangling everywhere and both the men wore huge conspicuous watches.

"My grandson, Michael," said Peter, shaking their hands.

Smiles erupted and a litany of German exploded around them. Helga enthusiastically hugged Mike, who looked for guidance to his grandfather. More hearty chuckles and layered language, mixed with a few English phrases engulfed the two as they were led to a waiting car. In a minute they were off through the streets, soon whizzing by parks and store fronts which displayed very sophisticated merchandise. People and traffic, minus the bicycles, were everywhere like in Amsterdam but the resemblance ended there for it was a decidedly modern city.

"This looks different than I thought," said Mike to Peter. "It's nice, I mean, sort of like home, you know American towns."

"That's true but it's not the town that I knew growing up. Now Germans are proud of this affluent city but I'd like to show you some pictures of the old streets when we get some time."

Peter thought about the contrast between his first home and his present one. The apartment house had been demolished a year after the war because the nearby bomb damage had affected the foundation, causing it to shift and sink, slowing leaning toward the street. However, with the extreme housing shortage, they lived in it for several months until the doors wouldn't open anymore and the windows cracked from the strain. Then they became eligible on the list for different accommodations. Even so, it took almost another year before one was available, forcing them to live in temporary quarters.

Mike asked, "When will we get to see your house, Gramps?"

"It wasn't a house. It was an apartment building and I'm afraid we won't get to see it because it's been torn down, long ago. We lived on the third floor, shared the one bath with the two families on the second. It was years before we had a place with our own bathroom, for six of us. Pretty special, huh?"

"Our house in Indiana had just one bathroom, too, Gramps. Mom was the only one who had trouble with that. I'd have to really go but she always wanted to take a long bath."

"She did the same thing when she was little. Probably a girl thing."

They drove to Peter's boyhood location where a row of straight modern buildings framed the street, many of which had display windows cluttered with summer sales signs reading "schlussverkauf". Most of the stores seemed to be specialty stores like luggage or china shops with people going in and out, carrying big plastic shopping bags. Above it all stuck out the high *Reinturm,* Dusseldorf's commination tower, a sure sign of modern life.

In a small square a fountain bubbled below a bronze abstract statue that had spoke-like appendages sticking out in several directions. It provided a convenient spot for several perching birds which looked casually about, noting with apparent amusement the hustle of the humans. Nearby benches held two teenagers smoking and talking, a lady reading a magazine and a man with arms crossed obviously waiting for someone. A video store was on the corner.

"Up there." Peter pointed to the upper story of a new building. "That's where it used to be."

On the ground floor of the actual site, the present Balkan restaurant with a large extended awning seemed to be doing good business, even in the morning hours. In front the occupied outdoor tables covered with red checked tablecloths were encircled with planters filled with flowers and evergreen topiary shrubs. Banners advertising *Dusseldorfer Alt* and *Dortmunder* Beers waved from poles but otherwise the signs were small and unobtrusive.

They got a cool drink at the restaurant, sitting indoors. It featured modern décor and televisions showing a soccer game between *Bayern-Muenchen* and *FC Schalke 04,* an old favorite of Peters. He remembered his dream team in the forties when Szeppan and Kuzorra were the big stars. Later on, during a trip in '79, while attending a game in Gelsenkirchen at the seventy-fifth anniversary of the team, he had actually seen the veteran Szeppan sitting in the stands above him. It had been a nice moment.

They watched for a while, Mike enjoying the action but

the cousins were anxious to move on. The blare of commentary mixed with the clang of dishes and patrons' laughs were unsettling for them. This would have been an experience from another world for the little boy who once lived upstairs. Here at this place, he had brought stolen coal for heating and run errands for the baker below, getting a few marks and some bread in return. He used to wait in the alcove between the windows for his friends to come by, later to spy on girls.

Upon leaving they glanced at the video store next door. Everything was sparkling new and clean - the street, the cars, the people and especially the windows. But seeing the place in his sepia memory, Peter found it disappointing. It was like looking at the stores at Woodfield Mall at home and he never liked to window shop.

Down the street had stood the Hartman Lighting and Electric store, the firm founded by Peter's grandfather, Josef Hartman, and his brother. The bombs had destroyed it and after losing his three sons, his grandfather had turned his interest over to his brother. He and his son Martin went on to rebuild after the war. Later, Martin's two sons, Peter's cousins, Johann and Emil, moved it to a new location and had great success with the booming German economy.

However, Peter saw that his grandson looked unmoved so they only spent a few more minutes, for it was strictly a present-day kind of place. Nothing here could bring the past back or alive to the boy, Peter knew. Nor could he understand the connection that Peter and his father, both expected to follow in the family business, would have had if war and circumstances had not come into their lives.

They drove on to Emil's home in the *Benrath* section of town where the lovely collection of streets and homes emphasized their apparent comfortable life style. The cousins chatted, recalling some of the memories of the old place and Peter nodded, feeling a lump in his throat.

Once inside, the adults settled down, talking but Mike spent time starring out the window at the luxurious garden, now engulfed in an afternoon shower. His grandmother would have liked it here, he knew, but he wished for the day to get over with. Later he went into a television room and watched a news program but without understanding the language, his attention wandered. He pulled out his sketch pad but couldn't find a focus so returned it to his back pack.

"We're going over to Johann's house now," said Peter, coming to get him. "He lives near the *Schloss*, that's the palace, and we can look around a bit. I used to roam around there as a kid, only it seemed like a hundred miles from our apartment then. We had to walk there and back, a good day's outing, but it was always nice to see Aunt Sophia and Johann."

The heavy rain had stopped when they arrived but the air was still very misty and humid as they walked on the grounds of the Rococo palace built in the 16th century, looking almost ethereal through the wet vapors. They met other walkers, all with extended umbrellas, making Michael wonder why they didn't all go indoors when it was so wet.

Johann smiled at the boy, understanding his questioning look. "It often rains here," he said, in apology for the inclement weather. He explained how Germans loved to walk and this was actually considered only a drizzle, a nice break for Dusseldorf. After a few minutes they decided to leave and headed for Johann's home nearby. His was an older two-story structure which had been two apartments in earlier times but he had long since converted it into one house.

After they had taken a tour of the house with Peter noting all the improvements since his last visit, Johann said, "I have something to show you that I found when we cleared out this old room in the basement. You know in the old days we used it as a laundry room and it's been a storage place ever since. I'll admit, I never touched a thing down here for years but I finally got around to fixing it up a bit. You see, over there, my brand-new wine cellar. I'm proud of it."

"We'll have to do sampling," laughed Peter.

"Absolutely," said Johann, winking at the boy. "A little soda, perhaps?"

Mike understood the idea and smiled back.

"But now, here is something that you can't believe." Johann pulled out a large crate filled with books, magazines, and photo albums. "These belonged to your mother, Peter. I'm sure she must have brought them here before she died and we forgot all about them."

Peter explained to Mike that his mother had come to live with them the last few months of her life. His own sisters had married and moved to Hamburg by then and their mother hadn't wanted to follow them, staying instead in familiar surroundings. He then picked up a couple of the photo albums, filled with scores of pictures.

"My God, look at this," exclaimed Peter. "I don't even know who all these people were," he said as he flipped through the pages. "Here, Mike. Now you can see in these old photos the old Dusseldorf, the way I remember it."

The boy started to page through the albums, finding the old photos of people and houses interesting. Johann served some wine and soon the men were laughing and filling their glasses again. They gave Mike a small soda and he settled on the floor, arranging the books. A clump of photos and clippings fell out of one of them.

"Look at this, Gramps. Are these people our relatives?"

Peter leaned over and examined a photo. "That man in the middle I think is my father," he said slowly. "I don't remember him very well because he died when I was little, you know. In fact, I only have two pictures of him myself but my sisters may have more. Johann, is this Father?"

Johann looked at the image also. "Yah, I think that's your father all right. Of course, I don't remember him very well either."

"But who are all of these? He's certainly with strange people, all dressed up in fancy customs. What in the world?" asked Peter with a startled catch in his voice. What and who were looking back at him from the photo? He had no idea and all the rest shook their heads also in mute response. It was certainly a party or perhaps Carnival, like good times before the war. So, Dusseldorf opened a glimpse, albeit yellowed and mysterious, for them into the past after all, thought Peter.

Later after storing the crate in their cabin, they joined the other tourists for a buffet dinner on the deck as the rain had stopped. Then the chorus group from Norway presented a concert again, mixed with favorites to please the older crowd, and a few more recent numbers. It was their farewell performance as they were going home the next day. Mike liked to see other youngsters perform. He clapped loudly as they finished and Peter saw him loosening up his reserve.

The late evening sky had cleared and the evening turned balmy. Peter, feeling unsettled by the afternoon discovery, wanted to stretch his legs before he returned to look at the photos again. "Let's go for a walk," he said as he glanced at Mike whose face mirrored some confusion about walking again.

"So, where are you going, Mike?" the piping voice of Kari the Carrot broke in, joining them.

"Ah, nowhere in particular," he said, a bit startled.

"Just a walk along the Rhine," said Peter.

"Good, that's just where I was heading."

"Now, Kari, are you sure we're not interrupting them?" said Julie coming up quickly. Her eyes flashed at them, suggesting an invitation.

"Oh, no," stammered Peter. "Join us if you like."

"That would be so lovely," she cooed.

Peter smiled but Mike looked uncomfortable. What a set-up, he must be thinking. Ahead of them, they spotted Emma the guide very engrossed in conversation with an older man. As they neared them, they stopped talking and Emma, suddenly turning, smiled at them.

"Having a nice stroll?" she offered. They all responded in kind but Peter thought Emma's voice seemed rather forced. The tone seemed anxious, making him turn around again. He heard them talk again but not in English. They had separated but he noticed Emma stashing an envelope into her tote bag as she quickly headed to the gangplank of the boat.

The others hadn't caught the language bit because Peter knew that for most monolinguals, all foreign languages tended to sound the same. He shrugged it off, for after all travel guides, especially the Dutch and Swiss, very often spoke many languages. No big deal and he had enough disturbing thoughts of his own. Those photos came back to him again. He wished he was alone now, letting the evening air clear his head and give him some solace but the babble of Karen and Julie engulfed them.

He half heartily joined in their conversation but didn't offer any sightseeing tips. As a boy, how often he had strolled along that river whose old cityscape was now gone. The replacement city was self explanatory to any observer but they'd find it hard to envision how it had been nearly leveled by the Allied bombers. His grey mood intensified when he remembered the smoking and smoldering buildings, the boarded-up windows, the glass and bricks splattered on the streets.

It started to mist again and he suggested that they return. Mike seemed to be enjoying himself, however, talking in earnest, to Kari. Later he was laughing at Kari's antics as she bounced up and down the street. She started splashing in the standing puddles and Michael joined her. Julie grabbed Peter's arm and giggled, pointing at the youngsters but he instinctively moved away from her. After a while the rain started in earnest, giving them all a good soaking as they fled back to the boat. Naturally, they had forgotten to take an umbrella.

Settling back into the cabin, Peter and Mike laughed as they stripped off their clothes and hung them up. Mike seemed animated and it broke the despondent mood for Peter.

"You know that Kari isn't really so bad after all, Gramps. The aunt is a bit flashy I'd say."

"You learned a lot in the rain. Even got over those braces, have you?" said Peter, waving his finger at him in jest. "You better watch out, young Romeo."

"She can't help that," said Mike rather defensively. Then looking at his grandfather who was pulling on his pajamas, he added, "You better watch out yourself. I saw you looking at the guide lady and then there is that Julie. Kari said she is quite the number, traveling all over, here and there. Some type of consultant. She gave you quite a once over, you know."

Peter laughed out loud. "Yah, yah, yah. I think your brain also got a little soaked, young man."

"I'm just looking out for Grandma's interest, you know," Mike laughed, whipping his towel at Peter. "She told me to take good care of you."

"Good. Good, you do that," said Peter, suddenly missing Margie.

The kid was joking, of course, but also observant. That Julie was rather forward and that could be annoying. But something about the incident with Kari while they were walking had caught his attention.

Suddenly little Marta, a childhood friend of his, came into his thoughts. Pert, wide eyed, and very smart, she lived down the street and sat ahead of him in their fourth-year class, her long brown braids dangling down her back and unto his desk. She was his only real competition doing math problems and was very outgoing, something like the red headed girl on the boat. They'd become friendly rivals, somehow thinking of themselves as different from the others. Though it was unthinkable to play outdoors with a girl at his age, he'd often watched her and her family coming and going from their first story apartment.

One fall day he noticed the doors were open with several people milling in and out, carrying cases and boxes. Seeing Marta standing alone outside, curiosity drew him to the house. Her big eyes were filled with tears and he knew without being told that something strange was happening.

"We're going to Canada," she said in a halting voice.

"Canada? With all the Eskimos?" His astonished reply didn't connect to the why or when, just the where.

"Father says it will be a better place, we'll be safe."

Peter frowned, lowering his eyes. His corner in Dusseldorf was his only world and he didn't understand a better, safer place. Only later did he realize that she was Jewish and their worlds were indeed becoming different. On a pleasant vacation trip to Canada in later years, he thought of them and wondered where they lived but he had never heard from them again.

"I think we better hit the sack. Sorry that Dusseldorf wasn't more interesting."

"Oh, it wasn't so bad," said Mike as he went into the bathroom.

Peter drummed his fingers on the table. The boy was doing OK, but of course, he hadn't gained any real perspective of his grandfather's life as a child. So? It was gone. He saw the crate and moved it under the bed with his foot, being tired and a bit chilled and not motivated to probe the contents. They will keep for another day, he thought. After all it's been more than fifty years since those pictures were taken and they can wait a while longer, he reasoned.

However, that night he had a dream where the old Dusseldorf appeared as he was stealing coal. It was night. Their apartment house, grey stucco with the aging dark green wood trim, the slender long windows, the tiny balcony where the family bicycle was stored, all seemed real. The baker's windows downstairs, now empty of bread and rolls. He saw the inside stair, shining polished wood with the rail painted black. The door to the apartment, opening with his mother in her heavy robe standing there, calling to him as he mounted the steps with his coal bucket, all appeared like a cloudy vision.

"Peter, did you get any coal?"

"Yah, sure. The British were sleeping early tonight. Klaus and I didn't have any trouble." It wasn't exactly the truth.

They hurried into the kitchen; the only warm place left in the house for they had run out of briquettes three days ago. They no longer used the bedroom or living room. His two sisters, wearing coats and gloves under the blankets, looked up from their cots on the floor. Their grandmother was asleep on the sofa pulled into the room, her white hair and face without her glasses on, just visible above the blankets. They quickly started the fire and he huddled close to the stove, thankful for another reprieve from the cold.

It had been raw outside that night, Peter remembered in this dream. His saw his friend, Klaus, and himself going down the empty street. No lights were shinning in the windows. During the war, they had black outs when they often went to the basement during the raids, but after the war, the nights seemed even darker. The planes and bombs weren't the reason anymore; now there wasn't fuel to waste on lighting rooms.

They discovered a hole in the fence that surrounded the train yards. An extensive network contained the long, loaded cars of coal coming from the nearby mines and was guarded by the occupying English army. This vast German underground resource which had so successfully fueled the Third Reich now moved to other destinations, not certainly to the heating stoves of the conquered.

Going after midnight made it safer, even as they knew it was dangerous. It wasn't too much of a trick for energetic youths to get past the occasional guard or flashing light. The challenge didn't come in scaling the coal car either but it all came down to noise. There could be no clatter of their buckets, absolutely no sound during loading. His only pair of gloves was needed, not only for the cold, but more importantly to muffle the noise as he slowly piled the treasure in the bucket.

So far, noise had not given them away but they goy spotted as they started to climb the train car. The waving light and scolding voice of the guard came from far down the tracks. They jumped down, instinctively slid under the car and came out on the other side, crouching low. They didn't want to openly head for their secret hole in the fence.

Waiting for the man to get closer, they took their chances. It worked out well as the man's searching beams signaled his course and as he crossed to the other side of the train, the boys were able to slip back once more under the car and get to the opening undetected. But they knew that their presence was suspected and that added risk. The dream seemed so real.

The dangerous crisscrossing of the flashlight in his sleep caused Peter to stir. Then his next dream came. From his tent, he saw the girl running and waving, shouting in Hungarian but he understood. The Serb partisans had entered the village. She had orange red hair and wore teeth braces, sparkling in the sun. Immediately behind her came horsemen, wearing turbans and flashing swords, also glittering with streaks of light.

No, that couldn't be right. This dream is all mixed up, in time, in place, in meaning.

He shook his head as he arose in the bed. Nearby Mike was sleeping. The light of the early morning filled the room. He felt the starting tug of the boat's movement. They were leaving the dock and going on down the Rhine to Cologne, he knew. They'd be there for breakfast and another tourist day of history and attractions would fill the schedule.

"Oh, my God, Margie," he whispered. "This trip is something else. I sure wish you were here. But I've got to admit, I'm rather intrigued by this see-saw adventure," he said to himself as he rolled over again and caught a few more winks of sleep.

COLOGNE (*KOLN*)

THE TRAVEL BOOKS of Cologne always began with a description of the well known and beloved symbol of Germany, the glorious cathedral standing near the Rhine, its twin spires visible for miles. Begun in the 13th century, it was finished only in the 19th and barely escaped destruction in the 20th. It is one of the world's largest Gothic structures and the sheer mass of its medieval facade, relieved by the lacy stone tracery around the huge stained windows, now looked down at the boat which slowly came down the river.

"Now there's a famous landmark, Mike," Peter said as they leaned against the railing, admiring the cathedral.

"It's so big, just like a skyscraper."

"The middle age equivalent of a high rise, that's for sure. Still dominates the city, doesn't it? The outside structure is majestic and there's a lot of great art inside too like the shrine to the Magi and a magnificent altarpiece. We'll see those when we go there. Probably even walk up the south tower to see the city, if you're up to it," he added, thinking he'd be the one tested on that stiff climb.

"Is all that stuff really old?"

"Yes, I would say so. The city itself was started by the Romans around the time of Christ. One can still see sections of those city gates in the old town and ancient remains in the archaeologist zone of the city. I once went to the Roman-Germanic Museum which is really interesting. In medieval times Cologne was the biggest town in Germany."

"How do you know so much about the place?"

"Well, every school boy in Germany knows about Cologne. And other important cities, like Heidelberg, too. We'll have a chance to visit quite a few important places on this trip."

"Sort of like New York or Las Vegas, everyone knows about them, right?"

"I suppose so," said Peter, laughing. His own viewpoint about Las Vegas was rather negative, certainly not typical of America but rather a fantasy desert version. New York, of course, offered many different cultures and fame but many thought "there was New York and then there was the rest of America". That example was also true for many big urban centers like Chicago and other metropolitan cities around the world. One couldn't get a sense of small towns or villages nor the rural landscape that lay beyond them. Unfortunately, their river cruise shared that same restriction too.

"But look there, ahead now. See that big bridge?" said Peter. "It's the *Hohensollern* Bridge and we'll be docking nearby. Up there, can you see that other big building, the railroad station?"

"Yah, but that one doesn't look so nice."

"You're right, not so pretty to look at, but never the less, important in recent times. Over fifty years ago, a thousand Allied planes peppered this place." It was in '42, not long ago using the European clock, but certainly considered history in Illinois. Peter was always amused when people went to see interesting places or buildings in Illinois, proudly pointing out that they were nearly a hundred years old.

"They completely destroyed that bridge and railroad complex, so what you see now are fairly new replacements." He paused only slightly in his delivery, as a quiet tribute to his many noisy nights of sirens and crashing buildings. "The bombers were aiming at important transportation targets which were the way for the army and supplies to cross the river."

"To knock out our enemy, right?"

"Right," said Peter slowly. His grandson's acceptance of their collective enemy came so naturally. He obviously still hadn't separated his grandfather of the present from the person of the past. Like himself at eleven, he couldn't know that one's sense of the enemy always depended on the angle that a person saw the threat. He couldn't ever have imagined that the land of the raiding bombers would become his home.

Continuing his explanation, "Just like in Dusseldorf, almost every building in this city was destroyed or badly damaged. At the end, just miles of rubble but…"

"But?"

"What do you think was left standing?"

"Oh, that's easy. The cathedral," said the boy. "You said it was built hundreds of years ago."

"That's right. Can you believe those RAF raiders were so good that they hit the train station, bull's eye, many times and dissolved it to ash? Can you see how close it's to the cathedral?"

"Yah. Across the street. They must have wanted to save it."

"You got that right. Hit all the surrounding buildings but they avoided the cathedral. It was their touching gift to a country where so many other historical buildings and churches fell to the shells of war."

The boat slowed as it cruised under the bridge and found its berthing place on the bank. After breakfast of more hard rolls, cheese and sausage, the passengers were eager and waiting to depart. Emma waved her umbrella and passed out her tourist brochures and then they were off in a sleek bus.

"Did you all have a good rest?" she inquired cheerfully. "We're going first to drive around Ring Street which follows the line of the old fortifications from Roman times that protected the city. Medieval Cologne, very close to the border, also needed significant protection in the days of warrior combat, as you can imagine."

She continued her history lesson and Mike listened even if his grandfather had already covered some of the basics. They saw the City Hall, the oldest public building in Germany and in passing heard the carillon bells ringing. A lovely sound. Emma told them that there were twelve Romanesque churches located in the city, all contributing it to be proclaimed a World Heritage Site.

They were diligently shown the famous cathedral, its solid soaring height impressive to them. The best feature for Mike was the hand carved, huge wooden doors with the strong iron braces. Emma explained that they were only opened on special occasions and he tried to imagine them swinging open and shut through the ages, allowing kings and bishops to come and go.

He started to sketch the doors. He found the smaller passageway doors the most interesting as they were cut into the larger ones. They were the openings that were actually used by the populace. For a giant, they might look like the little cat door his grandfather made in the garage door in Illinois.

Afterwards some slower passengers meandered in the place and some went browsing but Mike and Peter sat on the front steps and sipped a soft drink. They had decided not to climb the steps to the top of the tower. Peter then suggested they find a phone and he'd call his sisters in Hamburg. After a survey, they found one in an arcade nearby and he connected to both of them, chattering away about the trip, while Mike played a video game about some war battles.

"Come here and say hello," said Peter, interrupting Mike's concentration. He obliged but after a few muffled attempts at German, his grandfather relieved him.

"Thanks for trying. They are doing well. Too bad we won't get to see them. But now we must be off to see some more sights."

Mike asked, "There are sure a lot of these Heritage places."

"That's what you get from being old and needing preservation. Just like me," joked Peter.

The Cathedral bells rang out, piercing so loud that they could have used ear plugs. It continued for some time and when it was over, Peter said, "It's certainly a call to the faithful. My head is still ringing."

"Wasn't it a way to tell time, before watches?"

"True, it did that but I prefer those carillon sounds at the city hall."

Suddenly plopping down beside them was Kari, carrying a shopping bag with many colorful feathers sticking out the top.

"I bet you can't guess what Aunt Julie got me," she said teasingly.

"I can't guess, you're right," said Mike. "But I am curious. Did you perhaps kill a chicken for lunch?"

"Ah, you're guessing. But no, no. It has to do with Carnival."

"Carnival? I didn't see any carousel rides around here. Do

they have a shooting gallery, you know the kind where you hit the target and get a teddy bear or possibly a stuffed bird?"

"Not that kind of carnival, Silly."

Mike twisted his mouth. As much as he was starting to accept Kari the Carrot, he didn't like this superior tone.

Peter spoke in the interlude. "Cologne is famous for its Carnival. That's the big-time celebration before Lent, like the Madre Gras in New Orleans."

"Oh, now you've given him too big a clue," chided Kari.

Mike looked at the bag again, shaking his head.

"You're clueless, right?" said his tormentor, a bit more sympathetic. "It's kind of a tough one,"

Julie joined them and unknowingly ended the suspense. "Did Kari show you her mask?"

This prompted her niece to theatrically pull out a red and yellow decorated mask, topped by a headband of spectacular feathers. "Voila!"

"Isn't it something?" Julie continued, eyes flashing at Peter and her hand tugging at his shirt front.

"You actually aren't too far off, Julie," he said, a bit flustered, patting his shirt. "But fortunately, I'm not wearing a tie. That's part of the fun here when people celebrate *Weiberfastnacht.*"

"So, what's the *Weiber* thing?" demanded the curious Carrot.

"Ha, ha," Mike retorted, not knowing the answer either but finding a good wedge for revenge. "We got you there. I bet you can't guess."

"Michael, Michael, it's not a contest," said his grandfather in grandfatherly tone.

"Do tell us about Carnival, will you, Peter. You know so much about this place," the Carrot's aunt asked, sounding coy while digging for information.

"All right. As I said, it's their Madre Gras. Masks are big time features, as you can see, for Carnival is a costumed event," said Peter, his mind remembering a colorful night of merry making, when as a young man, he went carousing through the streets of Cologne. It had been a very special event for him, spending his few hard-earned marks to get there. He went with a group of older fellows and his friend Klaus, only recently released from the army and feeling their oats. Several of them were dressed up as pirates and he'd gone as a sheik. To his surprise, his mother had come up with a turban and a black mask, claiming his father had used them years ago during Carnival. Yes, the one in the photo album.

Peter cleared his throat, canceling his flashback. "Well, people really celebrate before Lent. It's not unknown for people to take out a loan so they can pay for all the meals and the costumes. Or at least, they did that when I was young. Probably now with their affluence that might be just an interesting dated detail."

"So, what's the *Weiber* thing?" demanded Kari again.

"*Weib* means wife or woman, and you can call it their special protest. The custom could be interrupted as a demonstration of warning or revenge. On the first Thursday they carry scissors with them in order to cut off the ties of men." The questioning looks of his audience prompted him to quickly explain. "They're used for some men who had, let me say, bad behavior during Carnival. Something like that."

"I hope they didn't do any serious harm," said Julie, taken aback, catching the meaning.

Kari chanted, "Oh, man, they could do serious harm, serious harm."

"It's viewed as very symbolic," Peter said in an obvious

adult tone. It was common knowledge that many judges turned their backs on divorce charges of adultery during Carnival, claiming it was only the result of merrymaking. He felt the urge to shock Julie with more information but he restrained himself. He couldn't get into marital infidelity in this setting. However, the youngsters started to mimic the shears' action with their fingers so probably they already had some general idea.

"Anyway, they all have a big parade, lots of fun, beer drinking, singing and horsing around."

"Horsing around," echoed Mike and the Carrot, their ready giggles showing the natural characteristics of their youth.

"The party goes on for days, and most people end up at a hangover supper of noodles and bread on Ash Wednesday," Peter continued, straight faced. "Then they repent and atone. That about covers it."

"What's a tone? Music?" asked Mike.

"No, atone, one word. When you're sorry for something you've done and you try to make up for it. Like when you left the water dripping all night long and it flooded some of the basement, remember? You had to clean it up."

The timing was right for a break as Emma, with closed umbrella twirling above her head, arrived and ushered the straggling group along the pedestrian walkway. She pointed out the Philharmonic Hall and then suggested they visit one of the nearby museums of their choice. Peter thought the *Germanishes* Museum would be a good choice for tourists but Julie wanted to see modern art pieces. Glancing at her guide book, she announced that one of the museums had a lot of Andy Warhols, her favorite pop artist.

"Oh, no," objected Kari. "We see them all the time at home."

You got it right, thought Peter. Why come to a foreign country and want your own duplicated? Julie agreed, surely not on the logic of that argument, but probably as a tactical move to stay with her companions.

They wandered down a small byway and came to the *Altstadt*, or Old Town. A city market was doing brisk business and they all browsed a bit among the vegetables and linens. A robust Turkish German was selling all sorts of electronics at a booth that fronted up to the 14th century Gothic *Rathaus*, or City Hall. Now that's a mix of time and cultures, certainly a revealing picture of present-day Germany, thought Peter. After the war, Germany, low on man power and in need of workers, encouraged immigration, especially from Turkey. What was thought a short-term solution proved to be a more long-term situation. After two generations, the Turks were still there and most were integrated into German life.

"This area has many pre-Gothic churches," he said, sounding again like a tourist guide or a teacher. "Over there is *St.Maria im Kapitol*."

"Just look at those carved doors," said Mike. He grabbed for his sketch pad.

"You certainly like doors, my boy, don't you?"

"Well, those doors take work, you know. I tried carving at my old school. I wasn't very good but I still liked it."

"I didn't know that, Mike. Perhaps you can try again when we get home. I've got a good workshop. We need something to dress up our front door. A fancy carved insert in the center panel would be nice."

"Yah, I suppose so." Mike looked down and Peter knew that he had hit a nerve of some kind in the boy. He wondered what it could be but then it came to him. Mike's father used to work at the local retail store selling doors and windows. He must miss him.

Mike had never complained or questioned them about his father's absence since the divorce. This had struck Margie and Peter as odd but they felt it was up to his mother to guide the boy and to convey the important information. An ironic factor stuck Peter now, given that he had not questioned much about his own father until this trip. Perhaps suppressed memories and questions can lay hidden deep. So deep for years.

"So, what else is there to see?" said Kari. "Let me look at your book, Auntie."

Scanning the pages, she announced, "Here's the choice. Some old church that has lots of religious stuff and corpses, or we could go to…"

Mike's head jerked up. "Hey, let's see that," he said, grabbing the book. "This one is cool," he said, scanning a picture. "He almost looks like a mummy, look at the ribs and those long bones for arms. Why do they save these guys?"

"It's a religious thing, Dummy," said Kari.

"Oh, goodness, isn't there something lighter, newer?" said Julie.

Kari yanked the book back. "Or here is the *Reinpark* that has a cable car. Also, the building has a canopied dance floor with a fountain on top."

"Sounds like fun," said Julie, her voice lilting like a waltz.

"I think that's too far to walk," said Peter quickly, sensing a trap.

"OK, then we have the, the *Ferm…Fermelde…*," read Kari.

"*Fermeldeturm*, that's the radio, TV tower," offered Peter.

Not intimated as she tried hard with the pronunciation, Kari tried again.

"*Fermeldeturm*. It's 794 feet high, near the *Stadtgarten*.

Probably like the one we have in Seattle, Auntie."

"It's pretty far, too, but we could take a cab," said Peter caving in. "We'll have to tell Emma that we won't be meeting her at the bus for the trip back to the boat."

"No problem," said perky Kari. "Just tell her we're doing our own thing."

Peter smiled at her young spirit of adventure, if not her galling confidence. So, they settled on the tower and as he hadn't ever been there before, he was glad to go and avoid the dance floor option. They went off in good humor, laughing and enjoying the sights and sounds. Being a tourist could be fun.

Only later when they were back at the boat did a troubling image bother Peter. Mike and Kari had gone out to scoop the scene, as they liked to call it, but promised to stay close. He rose, pulled out the crate from under the bed, and opened the photo book.

The dilemma bothered him as he started going through more of the materials. He'd have to find out more about Herman Hartman. Straining to get a sharper look at a photo, he saw a man with dark straight hair, strong build and amused face under the headdress that he had worn during Carnival. He wore a standard suit with an open collar in a relaxed pose. Not a bad impression for a father.

But the day had been long and in spite of the interesting faded faces, his eyes soon closed. His old muscles were tired. Mike returned to the cabin with a bang, waking him up. He'd had fun with Kari, spying on people on the deck.

"We even caught Emma smoking, sitting on a chair near the gangplank," Mike said. She was watching the nearby street when a man joined her, pulling up a chair and sitting very close to her. They had watched the couple from the shadows, not hearing the conversation but after a while, they both got tired and scampered back to their cabins.

"Gramps, guess what? I think Emma has a boyfriend. He's some guy we saw while we were out walking and he later joined her. They were talking, real close."

He stopped, seeing Peter asleep, sprawled out among the photos and books. "Well, I guess that news will have to wait until tomorrow. And you'll probably say it was wrong to be spying on them so I'll do this atone business right now," he said as he collected the articles, putting them in the crate and then carefully covering his grandfather with a blanket.

BONN

THE SMALL PROVINCIAL town of Bonn became the capital of West Germany after the war, influenced by the fact that the aging Adenauer, the first post war leader, lived nearby. In his youth, Peter had only known it as the birthplace of Beethoven, a special enough distinction actually, but one that had never warranted a visit before so he was interested in seeing it. Besides, any capital, past or present, was worthy of attention and it provided a morning stop on the guest's itinerary list.

"It may not look like it, but you're actually seeing where modern history was made here," said Emma. "An end of an era. Important events took place here. In this city they built a modern vibrant democracy out of a destroyed country, and recently the transfer of that very power happened on these streets. Germany went back to its roots, so to speak, because Berlin became once again the capital."

"It's when one town wins the championship and gets the trophy from the previous winners. Like the Stanley Cup, right?" said Mike, the perennial fan of the Black Hawks, no matter if they won or lost.

"That's about it," said Peter. "Passing the torch, you could say. Do you know why the change happened?"

"Sure, something about the wall and East Germany. Russia too."

"That's about right. They were the components of that turn of history, all right. This afternoon we can attend the lecture on the boat that is provided by the tour company if you want. They're talking about the modern Germany."

"Think they'll show pictures of tearing down the wall in Berlin?"

"It is possible. I don't know for sure. We'll see." For his part, Peter didn't need to hear the recent history regurgitated but as Kari joined them, it was amusing how they seemed to be hitting if off.

"She's sort of like me. She told me that her parents got divorced," Mike confided later to Peter. "Her Mom just got married again and is on her honeymoon to Bermuda, or someplace like that. Anyway, that's why Auntie took Kari on this trip."

"Yes, she said that when we met," said Peter.

"She says her aunt lives in London now but came back for the wedding. She said her aunt wasn't too thrilled to take her at first but it's working out. Even Kari thinks she is pretty unusual, always asking a lot of questions from people."

Peter laughed. "Unusual? That's a good word. Poor Karen must have got it from somewhere."

The tour bus took them past the modern government buildings. The Germans had initially planned for Bonn to be a temporary stop gap measure until Berlin could emerge as the new capital again. But the cold war and the wall, cutting off the Russian controlled eastern section of the country, ended that idea. The original buildings of the teacher's college were put into service and later augmented by additional neat and orderly functional structures.

However, West Germany's cities and landscape couldn't even be compared to the ugly government buildings and neglected countryside of the East. He remembered that rather fateful summer trip that he and Margie had made by train for a language conference through the eastern zone to Berlin.

Arriving at the border at Magdeburg on the Elbe River, they needed to switch trains. Immediately young East German guards, openly carrying their weapons, surrounded the cars. There was a lot of shouting, just to make sure that everyone knew that the military was present. From the side came barking trained dogs straining on their leashes. Their handlers freed them and they disappeared under and around the cars.

Even though Peter and Margie had already been checked at customs, a brisk young inspector came on board, opened their compartment and went through their luggage pieces again. His gruff nod and stiff turn were straight out of stereotyped war movies, the kind that Peter hated to see. But after he left, he smiled at the dreaded threat.

"What's so funny?" asked Margie. "The man made me mighty uncomfortable."

"It's just theatrical effect, don't you know."

"Did they think we had something to hide?"

"No, I don't think so. Just routine, they know we're Americans, always tell by the shoes. They're much harder on West Germans, actually, but they probably already had the high sign I'm German born. So that makes it a bit tricky sometimes."

"Well, I don't mind them going through the bags once but this guy was pretty abrupt." She reached up above her to the rack and pulled down a suitcase. "Oh, I didn't notice this," she said, opening the bag. "He did disturb things, mighty slick, I'd say."

"Just so he didn't make off with my speech and papers for the conference."

"Peter, I don't see them here. Are you sure you packed them in this case?"

"Well, of course."

"They're not here. Just look."

They both went through the contents, not finding the papers.

"Look again, Margie," said Peter with an edge of panic in his voice.

"Not here, Dear."

"Check the other one."

"That's mostly my stuff. Here, let's see." she said as he handed her the other suitcase. Neither bag contained his folder with his notes and the speech materials.

"Do you think they lifted it? How would they know and why would they care? My whole talk centers on language teaching techniques in America, especially multi-cultural influences. I'm not into bombs or spying."

"They might think it is just an excuse to be at the university, or perhaps the thing is some kind of code."

"Don't be silly. People come and go all the time through the zone to West Berlin. This can't be real."

"Where else did you put it? Could you have left it at Willy's place? You were reading it to him the other night."

"I'm sure I packed it, but then again, maybe."

"We can't find it here. That inspector was smooth but I can't imagine why they would lift something like that. You must have left it. We can't go back, we're on this train of no return, remember, no stops until Berlin."

"We don't have the time anyway. My appearance is already scheduled. God, what am I going to do? I couldn't possibly rewrite it. Besides, I don't have the bibliography to go with it."

He slumped down, his head hitting the window. "All this way, sponsored by the college, talking to an international conference, pretending that I'm the big expert and I lose my speech. Oh, God."

Margie saw his anguish and started going through the bags again. They didn't say anything. The clicking of the rails rang with a steady beat. Another short train passed them, going the other way. The late summer rural landscape floated by outside.

"What are we doing here?" said Peter, looking out with disgust. "Just look at that. These people are in the middle of August and they haven't started to pick up the harvest. The wheat is just lying there. Not a sign of a machine, not even a vehicle on the roads. No wonder they can't make their system work. In the West, grain is already in tidy barns and granaries."

"Peter, stop, for goodness sakes. Who cares about that now? You're just upset."

"That's for sure."

They both sat down as on cue. They stared out the window, speechless. As the train went around a rough bend; they could see the engine and front cars out the window. Suddenly the motion made his jacket fall down from the upper rack, spilling a folded wad of papers out of the pocket in the same moment.

"The speech!"

"The speech!"

They laughed and laughed, providing reason for several passengers going by the glass compartment door to stop and peer inside.

"It's all right, all right," said Peter, motioning them on.

Then they started to laugh again. It had been one of the dumbest things he had ever done but it ended with a noisy resolution. Perhaps a good moment on a train that didn't hear much laughter. Berlin held more memorable experiences but Peter laughed again at the thought of that trip on the train. Couriers sneaking forbidden documents or money to their contacts, indeed. Who ever thought of such a thing?

"Gramps, what's so funny?"

"Oh. Nothing, nothing. Let's see what they got planned for us this morning." He was back to the present. The tourists had a choice of sightseeing options again so Mike and Peter ended up going to the *Landes* museum where the big interest for the boy was the skull of the Neanderthal man. It was found near Dusseldorf in the 1800's but was dated back about 60,000 years.

"Well, that takes care of our forefathers, I guess. Check off anthropology. You interested in Beethoven's house?"

"Yah, sure. I suppose," said Mike. Peter was a bit agitated by his standard bland reply but it was at least not a "what ever", that totally irritating response of bored youth. He had to remind himself that the guy was only eleven. And besides, Mike had become more willing to go along with the programs, so that was good.

They had time for a quick stop at a restaurant which featured fresh Westfalen bread and clear oxtail soup with bacon and vegetables. A new one for Mike but it was delicious. At Beethoven's house a small quartet was playing in the background, providing a subdued atmosphere. The composer had left Bonn for Vienna as a young man but the displays showed many developments of his entire life. The most important ones were the ear trumpets that he used as deafness started to invade his world.

"Pretty amazing that he still could write music, and even symphonies, when he became deaf. All of it was in the head and heart, I guess," said Peter.

"Is that what you call a genius?" asked Mike.

"Yes, indeed, he was, but he sometimes had trouble with people."

"Well, that's better than being a cartoon. I always thought Snoopy invented Beethoven. Or vice versa."

"How about the Red Baron? Did you know that he was a real person too? And a German on top of it? Big flying ace in the first war."

"Yeah, he always had his scarf flying with the wind in the open cockpit. Just like Auntie. Pretty interesting, I guess, actually seeing some of this," said Mike.

Peter smiled, not bad progress after all. On the way back to the boat, Mike asked, "Are we going to see Berlin too?"

"No, not on this trip. Berlin is to the East, not on the Rhine or the Danube. But it's a pity we have to miss it. Lots of history there, past and present, to see," said Peter. He stopped himself from going on. Can't be too much of the professor, he thought.

"You ever been there?"

"A couple of years ago. The summer of '89, just months before the wall came down, when there was still an East and a West Berlin. Actually, I was just thinking about that trip I took with your Grandmother."

"So, was it exciting or dangerous?"

"Not really dangerous but somewhat uncomfortable at times, Mike. But looking back now, I could say it was quite a significant experience, seeing it was the end of an era and not knowing it."

"Why did you go there?"

"I was there for an international conference, talking about language learning. You know, that's usually when a lot of boring people attend boring meetings about boring topics."

Mike gave him a quick smile and Peter laughed. The definition wasn't too far off the mark either, he thought, as he remembered the event. Europeans at the time, still entrenched in their traditional formats, didn't understand his focus on multi-cultural teaching. That was before they knew about the needs of the refugee invasions.

"After it was over, we took a tour to East Berlin with the group and that was especially interesting for me. We had to go through Check Point Charlie to get there."

"What was Check Point Charlie?"

"A guard post with an entrance through the wall, manned by East German soldiers on the other side. They gave everyone a thorough inspection, luggage, papers in order, route of destination, that sort of thing. And sure enough, they had a guide there whose job it was, I'm sure, to also keep an eye on us."

"Did he act funny?"

"You could say there was some humor in it all right."

"No, I mean scary funny," Mike said, trying to get his point across.

"Well, he was pretty serious. We had to stop at a shop to change money. It also had tourist stuff, some packaged food, but most of the shelves were bare. You had to buy everything with their Eastern Mark. You couldn't exchange it back, either."

"What else did you do?"

"We saw the Brandenburg Gate from the other side. That's the big monument you always see as the symbol of Berlin, but was part of the wall then. We saw famous buildings like Humboldt University, cathedrals, the opera house and the old city hall. *Alexanderplatz* was a square that used to be the transportation hub of the city but what we saw was just an empty area, overgrown with weeds. It led no where, dead end. But those are places I had wanted to see all my life. Just driving down *Unter den Linden*, the most famous boulevard in Berlin, was really something for me. But a bit disappointing too."

"Why was that?"

"It literally means "under the Linden trees" because it was a famous beautiful shaded avenue with long lines of trees. That is, it was in the old days of the third Reich. And you can see the renewed boulevard again these days as part of the unified city but the forty some years in between, it wasn't quite up to that standard."

"It's like going to a place, say like Times Square, that you've heard about and it doesn't turn out the way you thought it was, right?" Mike laughed at his own comparison.

"Right on, my young man," said Peter.

"So, what was so funny, I mean strange?"

"Well, here in the bus sat older folks, the academic types from all over the world as this young guide pointed out the landmarks in a real packaged delivery, full of propaganda containing every socialistic fact and figure you could imagine. I'm afraid we weren't a good audience. We just smiled and some even laughed a bit."

"What's socialistic?" Mike asked.

"The communistic line, how well their government works, how that system does so much for the people. We weren't buying it, of course, even if we appreciated our own government that fortunately supports many programs for us."

"I still don't get why it was funny." Mike was frustrated.

Peter sensed the generation gap at understanding. "We

all knew it was a lie, all polished up for the tourist. It's like a movie set where you only see the store fronts. If one looked down the streets, everything was shabby, unpainted. Fake, an illusion. Of course, we didn't stop but the guide told us we would be getting out to see the highest point of interest, the Russian War Memorial. It's a park that displays the first Russian tanks to enter Berlin in the war."

"I'd like to see a real tank. That would be really cool."

"Oh, I agree. But it was raining and when the bus stopped, there were some quiet whispers and more coughs. The poor young man, probably really a decent kid just doing his job, jumped out of the bus and eagerly waited for the group to descend. But no one moved. He came back in, pretty concerned, giving his pitch again so a few folks shuffled out with their umbrellas."

"Did you go?"

"Actually not. I had seen my share of tanks in the war, Mike. I didn't need to see a communist monument when they didn't even allow us to walk freely down the street."

"So that was it? That was Berlin?"

"Oh, no, no. You got me off on a wrong tangent. West Berlin was different. You know, busy with people everywhere, buying, selling, very much like any other city. But we can't do justice to the place, either then or now, unless we have a lot more time to talk about it. Nowadays it's all one big city again and the capital of the country too."

"Did you like Berlin?"

"Yes, indeed. It's a great place. But that's a story for another time. We better hurry back."

Upon arriving at the boat, they saw everyone scurrying on board for it was time for departure. Carrot bolted out of the crowd and grabbed Mike by the arm. "You should have been with us. I saw her again."

"So, what was she doing?" he asked.

"Talking to a different fellow. Real close like," the Carrot answered, giggling.

Julie, hearing the remark as she also emerged from the group, leaned over to Peter and whispered, "You know, she's got a guy in every port."

Peter paused, "She? Who's she? Carrot? Or I mean Karin, Kari?"

"Heavens no! I'm talking about Emma, the guide, of course," said Julie.

"Oh, Emma," said Peter, plainly annoyed as he hustled Mike toward their cabin. "Really now, those two are a bit much. Don't they have anything better to do than to stalk our guide? *Sie faellt auf den Wecher.*"

"What's that mean, Grandpa?"

"It means someone is really getting on your nerves, like an annoying alarm clock ringing."

"But there is something going on with Emma. Kari and I saw her…"

"Hey, stop. I'll have to accuse you both of being bratty little kids, spying on people, making things up. Let's just stick to the program, Ok?"

Mike looked down, "Yeah, Kari really does have an imagination."

Peter mumbled, "And that Julie, can be a pain in the ass. Always snooping."

"What was that?"

"Oh, nothing, nothing. We're going to Koblenz this afternoon. The boat is moving already."

Mike stretched out on his bed, played with his watch and briefly scanned a brochure. He looked bored. "I hope we get to eat pretty soon," he said.

"There's a lunch buffet on deck, I think," Peter said, but added. "You go ahead, if you want. But don't get into any trouble." He knew the nice chatty history lesson with the boy had taken a sour turn and there was no need to pursue it.

They'd be passing Remagen soon where in 1945 the Allies crossed over the only surviving bridge spanning the Rhine, the last natural barrier into the heartland of Germany. They'd see lots of bridges on a river cruise.

"Probably I should get a bite to eat too," said Peter as he left the cabin. On deck he encountered Emma, who immediately recognized him.

"Oh, you're the man with Mike, the grandson. From Chicago, wasn't it? I'm supposed to remember all of that," she laughed.

"*Yah*. From Chicago. I'm Peter Hartman."

She paused a moment and her eyes searched his face. "But tell me now, it hasn't always been Chicago, has it? Or no, let me guess where you were born."

"The world is big," he said teasingly. She had drawn him in. Most people didn't identify his accent readily but the Dutch were terrific linguists and he knew she had lots of experience with tourists.

"Well, your name…"

"Names can be deceiving."

"Yes, yes," she said, looking him over again. He appraised her also, noting she was older than he had previously thought. "Your face and voice, your accent…"

Peter smiled at the appraisal. So much like Margie's years ago when she had confided to him that his most appealing quality was his voice, his accent, not typical heavy German but "continental" as she called it – smooth, sophisticated and even mysterious. It wasn't as good a trait as being handsome, he thought, but it had to do. Actually, he had worked hard on his diction, even doing acting in his college days, and it proved to be a helpful asset as a language professor.

"I'd say you were from Northern Germany? Or the Ruhr. Probably near here, right?"

"Right," he said, smiling. His sophisticated accent wasn't so mysterious after all.

"And why did you bring your grandson?"

"To see the world," he said, thinking of Julie. "Especially the river cruise down to Budapest. I took that trip when I was his age."

"You know that area then?"

"Yes, I spent a little time there, far south of Budapest actually, very near the border. It was Hungary in '43 but became Yugoslavia, and now I don't know for sure what it is. The land was beautiful, anyway in my memories."

"Yes, it's beautiful in memories," she said with a hint of sadness in her tone, as she turned. "I hope you enjoy the cruise. Let me know if I can ever do anything for you."

Peter ambled over to the buffet table. Steaming potato pancakes and tiny pork sausages appealed to him and fixing his plate of food, he sat down at a small table near the railing and gazed out at the lovely river scene passing by. He smacked his lips in appreciation of his good glass of Rhine wine. The flat country of the lower Rhine had disappeared and now a chain of seven steep hills, capped by *Drachenfels* Castle, came into view.

Here it was that legend said Siegfried, the hero of the Ring saga called the *Nibelungenlied* killed the dragon that lived on the rock. He bathed in the creature's blood and that made him invincible, except for an area on his shoulders where a leaf had fallen while he bathed. Too bad modern heroes didn't have dragon's blood to give them such powers, he mused.

A pensive mood engulfed him. He thought about the ancient heroes and landscapes so beautiful in memories. But he had misled Emma. His memories, not entirely dimmed by time, weren't always beautiful.

KOBLENZ

THE MOSEL AND the Rhine meet in Koblenz at what has been described as Germany's most beautiful corner, the *Deutsches Eck*. It is a promontory jutting out at the confluence of the rivers and has greeted many captors over time. The early Romans founded it in 9 B.C. and it reached its greatest power in the Middle Ages. Later French refugees settled in the area during the French Revolution. However, now it welcomed the tourist ships which docked at the riversides.

Emma led the group up to the equestrian statue of Emperor William I which caped the paved triangular park. "Here is where Bismarck announced the unification of the thirty-two princely states in 1893 to form the modern country of Germany, so you can understand why it's a significant historical site. The city of Koblenz, which was heavily damaged in the Second World War and now rebuilt, surrounds you. Across the river, 400 feet above, you can see *Festung Eherenbrietstein*, which was once Europe's largest fortress. Built in the tenth century, destroyed and rebuilt in the early 1800's, it could house 1500 soldiers and could withstand a six-month siege. Every August there is a fire-works show from the towers that is one of the grandest in the country."

"Can we go there and look it over?" asked one of the group.

"Yes, it's one of the choices we have here. You can take the ferry over the river and the gondola up to the castle. It also has a museum, restaurant, and a visitor center. Or you can take the short excursion down stream to the *Marksburg,* an authentic 13th century stronghold. It's the only castle on the Rhine which hasn't been damaged or renovated and gives a person the true sense of medieval life along the Rhine. We'll see many other castles as we sail along the river, but these two are the only ones where you'll have time to explore. Or another option is a walking tour of the Old Town of Koblenz. We'll also see the prince-elector's palace called the *Residenzschloss* and take a stroll along the river promenades. There are good restaurants, jazz clubs and places to shop."

"That last choice sounds good to me," spoke up Julie.

"And the *Marksburg* is a place I've always wanted to see," said Peter quickly. He didn't want to get stuck with Julie again. "What do you think, Mike?"

"Sounds good to me," he answered in response to his grandfather's not so gentle nudge.

"We'll have three hours for your excursions so people make your choices, and sign in here. I'll take the city group and we have local guides to assist you with the others tours," said Emma. Seeing Peter sign in for the *Marksburg* tour, she added, "Too bad you won't be able to have *Deppekooche* with us."

"What's that, Grandpa?"

"Oh, a potato casserole dish. It's good, all right."

Emma smiled. "The Max and Moritz Grill is always a favorite stop. Its where naughty kids stole the chicken and a dog got blamed for it." She winked at Mike.

"Sure you won't change your mind?" said Julie, with Carrot coming up beside them.

"No, I think we're off to history instead," said Peter.

"You'll miss seeing the *Schangel*," laughed Emma.

"What's that?" inquired the ever-curious Carrot.

"It's actually the city's mascot. A bronze statue of an impish figure who was always full of pranks, just like you two kids." Peter saw Mike squirm a bit. Perhaps Emma had noticed their youthful surveillance of her after all.

The *Marksburg* was impressive. From its beginnings in the 1200's as a protection of the city of Braubach, its crucial placement on the shore presented a romantic picture of historic beauty. The structure was noted for it three corner foundation, making it less vulnerable to attack. The great battery rose before them and they needed strong legs as they climbed the steps carved out of rock.

Additions had been made in the 16 and 17th century which included the high imposing tower which contained the chapel and living spaces below. It was the place of last refuge when the castle was overtaken. They would burn the wooden drawbridge leading to the chambers. Above them was the slate roof, which had been covered with plaster to protect the soft slate. They inspected the cannons which shot balls that were covered in smooth lead and could travel the entire distance across the river.

"Look at this," said Peter, pointing out the murder hole where boiling pitch would be poured down upon invaders. "They also had another hole opening to the ground below. It hung over and beyond the wall itself. It was such a vulnerable spot that the people were often locked in the room. Can you guess what that was?"

"Some sort of escape route?" said Michael.

"Yes, you could say that, and in some cases, it was used for that but it's usually called a toilet. Their only means of disposing their waste. It fell down to a garbage pile below."

"Oh, not too pleasant a landing. Carrot would call that really gross."

The display of weapons in the Hall of Knights immediately impressed Mike. In addition to swords, shields, and armor, they saw stone balls swinging on a rope and a battering ram. Now preserved as a museum with period furniture and affects, the large room was where most of the eating and sleeping of the knights was done. Also talking and arguing because the spaces of the castle would be very tight during bad weather and sieges. They almost could hear the long ago rustling of weapons and babble of the men.

Only the owner, his family and important guests would be able to have private quarters. It was also the only directly heated area in the castle and their windows would be covered with thin skinned animal hides, which prevented heat from escaping and allowing some light to penetrate the space.

Coming to the kitchen, they saw a great stone hearth which was big enough to roast an entire ox at one time. Because water was impure, the wine cellar below supplied the entire fortress with drinks. The wall was hung with pitchers on pegs for each person's allotment. Understandably this room and food storage areas were heavily guarded.

Going up the spiral staircases proved tricky because they were always made to turn clockwise, which favored right-handed defenders during battle. Then Mike hit his head on the door frame. "We can barely get through these doors," he moaned. "Why are they so low?"

"Remember people were much shorter back then. And besides any opening was considered a possible hazard, so they kept them as small as possible. They also didn't have steel beams to support weight so they had to work with the size of stones that they could manage."

The dungeon was the most remarkable room for Michael. Its small space displayed various torture devises. The guide told them that often with prisoners just the sight of them lead to confessions, whether real or otherwise. No one needed to tell the people of the time what the results were. Besides the hand and leg cuffs, there were several specific instruments that proved interesting.

The guide pointed out a metal mask with a heavy ball attached. "This was used for the gossipmongers, an apparent deadly trait of the time. They were accused of spreading false rumors, possibly secrets or vital information."

"It could apply to kids too, I'm sure," Peter laughed. "Anyway, people had to crawl with their nose in the mud with this on."

"And what's this?" Mike asked the guide.

"One of our best attractions. The chastity belts. They actually did exist, young man. You know the husband wanted his wife to be faithful, especially when he was gone for a long time, off to some distant battle or campaign. Now it is felt that women wouldn't like this sort of thing but there is evidence that on occasion it proved to be a very valuable defense item against unwanted advances. Or when they traveled through the country, even escorted, there was always danger of attack, so it provided some protection from various wanton acts," said the guide, looking a little uneasy at Mike.

"You probably should put it up with the weapon display," laughed one of the tourists.

Peter smiled in spite of himself but said to Mike, "I think it's time to take a break."

Outside, sitting on the low wall, looking across the Rhine, Peter took some photos. Mike suddenly asked, "So, why did they have to do it?"

"Do what? Go on campaigns? Build these fortresses? What?"

"No, no. Why did my parents have to split?"

Peter blinked. Here was Mike, who had enjoyed himself during the tour and now was sitting in a spot of spectacular beauty, far removed in time and place from modern America, having thoughts of home. A home so recently disrupted. A heartbreaking question.

"Didn't they talk to you, explain things about the divorce?"

"Not really, Grandpa."

Peter coughed. "I'm like you, in the dark about some of that. But I think it was that they got tired of being unhappy."

"My friend Josh said his folks seemed unhappy. They fought and screamed a lot."

"So, did they get divorced?"

"No, not yet, anyway. He called me a few days before we left and talked about my old school and stuff, but he didn't say much about them. Even you and Grandma argue sometimes."

"Disagree. But we aren't unhappy, Mike. It's just a hearty difference of opinion, that's all," said Peter, clearing his throat. They'd have to modify their language, he reminded himself. Another task on the growing list for them to master. Ah, to be the sandwich generation, the caregivers on both ends.

"But that's what is strange. Mom and Dad never had fights."

Peter thought, they had nothing to fight about, nothing to interest them, probably too bored with each other. Their marriage died because it was dead already. But the problem remained, how do you explain this behavior to an eleven-year-old? Did his parents marry too young, develop different agendas? It sounded like the modern maudlin excuses for incompatibility, not valid reasons for divorce to his satisfaction, and certainly not for his grandson. He didn't want Mike to be a fatherless child; he knew what that meant all too well and a grandfather wasn't a complete substitute.

"Mike, people can also be very unhappy, being quiet. Right? You're often pretty quiet and don't you feel unhappy sometimes?" said Peter cautiously.

"Sure, at times."

"Then you can probably understand their being unhappy." This was coming out pretty lame, but Peter didn't have any other direction. "Your Grandma and I are sad about this too. But there is one thing that we do know. We love you and we're all going to get better and be happy, right?"

His homey and admittedly feeble advice made him smart inside. Mike didn't respond. Questions whirled in his head. Life, love, marriage? For better or worse? Happiness? He knew the answer for himself. It wasn't one or the other; everything in life had some better and some worse to it but as a professor and grandfather, he was supposed to know the right, the definitive answers. Oh yes, right. How many times can he say right?

He thought of himself as a compromising realist, even if he knew that he was a bit pessimistic. Margie sometimes used words like avoidance and denial when describing Peter's approach to problems. At times she was the opposite; she'd talk and analyze too much but she had boundless faith that things would usually work out for the best and they usually did. It was really amazing. He admired that and knew their differences gave their marriage balance. And happiness? He felt he was a happy man, knowing that he'd had good fortune in marriage and because he could accept limitations without despair.

It was time for them to leave and join the others on board. From here the Rhine was the grandest and unspoiled. No more bridges until Mainz but there would be castles, castles and more castles. That should deflect the sadness of Mike for a while.

"Let's be on the lookout for more castles," Peter said to Mike and Carrot when they were again all settled on the top deck of the Majesty. The valley walls sloping up from the river were a patchwork of orderly vineyards and small exquisite towns with church towers and ramparts sticking out of the foliage. The road and train tracks that ran along side the river often disappeared into tunnels or tree cover. Busy river traffic of boats and barges passed them, coming and going.

"The place sure is busy," said Mike.

"Always has been. And it caused lots of conflict through the years, let me tell you. That's why there are so many castles. Each one protected a portion of the river and they demanded tolls. Do you see those two ruins up there? *Sterrenberg and Liebenstein*. But they had a different story, a different fight. Legend has it that there were two brothers. They fought each other so much that they built a wall between their castles."

After a big twist in the river, they saw *Burg Maus* ahead. "Take a look over there," shouted Peter.

"So, what's the story with that one," asked Carrot.

"Well, it was built…"

Emma's voice over the boat's microphone interrupted him "Further upstream we will see *Burg Maus* which was a Bishop's castle, and then *Burg Katz*. The further one was built in the 14th century by a count named *Katzeneinbogen*. He also owned the *Marksburg*, a place some of you saw. He was very proud of his castle but made fun of the Bishop's castle. He said he was the *Katz* or the cat and the other one was the mouse. That proved to be so appealing to people that both castles have those names to this day."

"I think I like the Katz castle," said Mike.

"So now where's the Cheese castle? Didn't anyone think of that?" Kari asked.

"Not yet, but don't tell Disney. They may invent one. Anyway, we're coming to the *Lorelei* soon," said Peter.

"What kind of castle is that?"

"Oh, no castle this time. It's a big rock formation on the side of a bend in the river. Actually, it is a dangerous place for the river boats to navigate. A siren once lived on top and lured the poor sailors to their death because they were so mesmerized by her song that they crashed into the rocks below. Poems and songs are written about it. Another German legend, I'm afraid."

"I think I get the idea," said Mike.

"It sounds more like a good excuse for their poor navigation," said the crisp condescending Carrot.

They continued on, rounding the *Lorelei* rising above them. Modern day excavation on the rocky shoreline and getting rid of hidden underwater rocks had proved to make it much safer for ships to cruise the watery passage. Later on, they saw Peter's favorite spot on the Rhine. *Die Pfalz* was a unique toll fort built on a small island in the middle of the river. It actually looked like a stone ship with a tower and a sharp stern which parted the river on both sides.

"I've always wanted to visit that place," said Peter as they passed close by. "It's like a small gem, but actually quite powerful. So much so that it was never overtaken by outside forces."

They settled back and watched the passing landscape with more castles and ruins on the cliffs above. Peter enjoyed the sound of the lapping water and thought about his days on the water, usually in a sailboat. Though he thought of himself only as a Sunday sailor, often going with friends from school, he'd become skilled on the water. He'd resisted buying a sailboat himself, even with the considerate approval of his wife, mostly because of cost and trouble of storage but also because she no longer fared well on the water.

During their courting days, they'd often gone out together in a rented number from Montrose Harbor in Chicago, looking at the skyline and dreaming of their life together. One afternoon, the romantic interlude had been seriously broken by her urgent need to go to the bathroom. Naturally at awkward times like that, there wasn't any wind when they needed to get into harbor, only enough to lap the water against the side of the boat, the sound adding to her distress. He laughed and she became embarrassed, escalating the desperate situation. They finally made it to shore all right, but somehow her enthusiasm for sailing diminished after that.

He remembered one fourth of July when they were stuck in the harbor because of high winds. They decided to make a relaxed day of it, soaking up the sun and eating their picnic lunch on board while watching the air show going on above them. However, fate was against them. The halyards of the docked boats clanged and clanged with the wind, the wine and food didn't sit well and Margie developed a gigantic headache that lasted for several days. Later, on bigger ships she often got sea sick, even with taking pills and more than once barfed over the side. Her participation really waned then but she always urged him to go sailing, knowing how much he enjoyed it. Thinking about it now, he realized how understanding she had been. But he was sure that she would have enjoyed this river cruise because it didn't include significant waves.

Another island was coming up, close to the entrance of the Nahe River into the Rhine. Peter remembered a fun time he and Margie had along the river banks while visiting his family years ago. They had stopped at small charming villages which produced incredible wine from the surrounding vineyards. The wine was not as well-known as others because there was a limited supply and wasn't usually found outside of the area. Perhaps the uniqueness made it so special but he remembered that time with fondness. Perhaps also it was because they were young. Ah, so young and so in love.

The guide's voice broke into his thoughts. "Now you see the island ahead with that slender tower and we have another mouse story. It is a bad story. Bishop Hatto, who controlled it, was known for many injustices such as burning beggars and demanding grain in time of drought. Even the mice hated him and when he sailed to this island refuge, they followed him and ate him alive."

"Cool!" shouted Michael.

"These legends are getting worse with every passing castle," said Karen.

"Well, we're almost to Rudesheim, that town coming up on the opposite bank," said Peter. "It's where we are to stop, according to our itinerary. Also explore the town and have dinner off the ship."

"Oh, good. Food," said Mike.

Rudesheim didn't disappoint them either. It was crowded with tourists but small enough for the group to explore independently. It offered interest to music lovers and the guide recommended going to see the mechanical music museum, showcasing inventions prior to the record player, tape or radio. If wine was one's passion, a wine museum was housed in the *Bromsergurg*, a splendid local castle.

Peter was interested in all the sights, especially the historic *Niederwald* Monument, a massive figure of Germania celebrating the country's unification after victory from the French in 1871. One needed to take the cable car high above the town and river to see it. It would have been a great experience, but Mike was hungry as usual and the pungent smells of the *Drosselgasse*, a narrow-cobbled street filled with restaurants and gift shops, lured them in.

As part of the famous wine district in Germany, Rudesheim provided the ideal setting for fine eating so Peter was happy with the smoked pork loin and dumplings he ordered while Mike got roast beef with horseradish sauce which he surprisingly liked. Just as they settled down, a man from the cruise paused by the table and Peter recognized him. They nodded to one another and Peter introduced himself and Mike.

The man said, "Good to meet you. I'm Roger Twilling. Nice town, isn't it?" He smiled and walked away.

Julie also came by with Kari. "Hello there. How are you doing?" she said.

"Fine, fine," said Peter, then hesitantly added, "Would you like to join us?"

"Oh, no, thank you. We just finished. I'd like to see more of this town with some folks from Dallas I just met."

Kari blurted out. "Oh, Auntie, can I stay here and talk with Mike?"

"Of course, dear little Carrot. I hope that's all right with you, Peter."

"Certainly. We'll be going back to the ship pretty soon."

"I'll pick you up later," Julie said to Kari and she was off into the crowd twirling her scarf.

After dinner Peter and his youngsters meandered around a bit before returning to the Majestic. Suggesting Mike and Kari visit outside on the deck until Julie returned, Peter settled down in the cabin to read the ship's newsletter and found news about Bosnia. It was not impacting most of Europe but it did give a disturbing splinter into the peace of the Balkan region. Ethnic and cultural differences still raising turmoil.

He couldn't stop remembering the past as he prepared for sleep. He was back there again in Dusseldorf. The war was still going on and he had endured another year. But then they arranged for him to leave again, this time to a farm family near Munster. Little choice. There he was expected to help and didn't appreciate milking cows and cleaning the barns. There weren't any companions nearby and he was homesick. Walking what seemed miles to school in the snow was another problem but he knew he was fed and safe.

Another winter passed and then spring finally came and with it, a bad case of the measles. However, this proved to be a fortunate event, because it delayed his induction into the German fighting force which was now desperate enough to enlist boys. Two months later the war was over and he was no longer needed in the Army of the Third Reich. He had endured many of the war's ravages but for the rest of his life, he was thankful to have luckily avoided that particular circumstance.

He rolled over, time to go back to sleep. His present reality of a lovely river cruise was far more comforting.

HEIDELBERG

THE BOAT CHURNED onward, until docking in the morning at Mainz. Peter had previously arranged a day bus trip to Heidelberg from this point so it meant an early departure from the boat with Mike. They would have a different tour leader for this excursion but they would join the Majestic again later. Carrot and company were not in evidence as they boarded so apparently, they hadn't booked the trip. Peter felt rather relieved but Mike looked around for them.

"So why are we going to this Heidelberg place?" asked Mike.

"Because it's famous. The city with Germany's oldest university."

"Oh," he said slowly, "So, I guess it'll be interesting for a teacher type like you."

"I'm sure you'll like it too, Mike," said Peter, trying to be convincing.

The bus rolled on. Probably because of the early hour and less interest, Mike was soon fading and falling asleep, head bouncing back against the seat. Peter found himself nodding too and was surprised when the bus stopped and they were in Heidelberg. A new driver came aboard, followed by the guide for the drive-by city tour. He began his introduction to the city as they wound through the historic streets with glimpses of the huge castle ruin rising above them.

"Welcome to Heidelberg. Heidelberg is our oldest and most famous university city and has often been described as the country's most beautiful city. You can judge that for yourself but I'm sure you agree that the setting is lovely with the Neckar River below and the surrounding wooded hills. People have lived in this area for at least a half million years, as evidence from the Heidelberger man's jaw bone that was discovered nearby in 1907 and identified as the oldest human sample of European life."

Mike said, "I wonder if he was related to that Neanderthal guy?" Peter frowned and then remembered their earlier lecture. The boy was pretty sharp, after all, to connect that information.

"Later in the 5th century came the Celts to the region and by the 12th century it was an important town. The castle which we are going to see shortly was begun in 1214 and considered an important Renaissance fortification and residence of the Palatinate rulers," said the guide. "As we get to the ruins, I'll give more information about the glory and tragedy of our famous landmark."

Mike said, "This guide isn't half as interesting as Emma."

"Well, I think he's doing a good job with lots of information."

The bus rolled by the Holy Spirit Church with its tall spire accenting the town. The guide continued. "This main house of worship has had an interesting history, especially during the Reformation and Thirty Years War, it actually served both Catholic and Protestant congregations at the same time. Later the Catholic court moved to Mannheim."

"Ahead, we'll be crossing the Main Street, or *Hauptstrasse*, of Heidelberg. It's the longest pedestrian zone in Europe and you'll see people on their seg-ways darting in and out. You might like to visit it later. It's an easy place to spend your money with shops and shops galore."

"So where is this university they talk about?" Mike asked Peter.

"Most of these buildings you see here are part of the old complex," said Peter, knowing Mike expected to see some sort of central campus location like most American educational institutions. Even Hawkins College was distinctly set off from its suburban neighbors.

The guide continued right on cue. "You now see the many buildings of the University, some dating back hundreds of years. But that is not all, many modern extensions exist throughout the city. All told, there are around 30,000 students, both from Germany and world-wide. The university museum is worth a visit, especially the Great Hall on the 2nd floor."

"And of course," the guide chuckled. "There is the student jail with walls covered in graffiti and slogans. For years, it was actually used to restrain disorderly students and names of the offenders still remain scribbled on the walls. Later it became a social outlet used for partying, which is still considered a trademark of the college crowd and an interest to tourists."

"Oh, I'd like to see that, Gramps," said Mike.

"I'm sure we can do that this afternoon when the city tour is over. But you have to do a favor for me too. Go with me to the Philosopher's Bridge."

"How can a bridge be for a philosopher?"

The guide again came in on cue. "We are now driving by the Karl Theodor Bridge with its thick red sandstone supports and named after the Palatinate Elector and Duke of Bavaria.

At the entrance is the medieval gate with two towers and an unusual decoration of stripes. Beyond is the promenade for walking and years ago, the academic philosophers of the university would take their strolls here and stop to contemplate the issues of the day, the big questions of the universe, the ethics of mankind and all those weighty questions. Now people of all backgrounds often do the same thing there."

"We'll be driving up to the castle where you can enjoy your time exploring the complex on your own. However, before you immerse yourself in the past there, let me say a few words about recent history. Unlike most German cities, Heidelberg fortunately survived both world wars without damage but it played a big role after World War II. Of course, American tourists know of the allied occupation of Germany. For years Heidelberg has been the headquarters for the US Army and NATO Command Center in Europe. Nearly 20,000 soldiers were stationed here. Obviously, this made a big cultural and financial impact on our city."

The bus wound up the hillside to a parking lot at the castle ruins. The tourists gazed out the windows, moving in their seats with anticipation. Mike's eyes were wide open and he turned to his grandfather with excitement.

"Too bad Carrot has to miss this. It's awesome."

"Just wait, you haven't seen anything yet"

The guide heard the interchange and nodded. "Before I let you go, let me give you some guidelines. Originally there was an upper castle and a lower one but the upper was destroyed. Afterwards the lower one was fortified and additions made. It has a long history of conflict. The French lay siege to the castle in 1689 and there's been many attempts to restore it but it was a tremendous task as you can see."

"Lightning even struck it twice causing a big fire the day

before Karl Theodor was to move into it. He gave up and went to Munich to establish the Bavarian capital. It was basically abandoned with only a portion of it restored later. Its commanding presence, however, remained and has emerged as the romantic symbol of this city."

Peter added seriously, "People like Victor Hugo and Mark Twain wrote about it, making it famous world-wide. You know many important people come here to see this."

"Yah, I do know that." Mike laughed. "We're here, right?"

The guide said, "Be sure to watch your steps as you wander about," he cautioned as the group departed. "But don't miss the *Heidelberger Tun* in the restored rooms. That's the large wine barrel containing 50,000 gallons of wine."

Mike set immediately to sketch the rising walls with empty windows framing the sky. He saw the skeleton of rooms, exposed to the world, with vines and vegetation making a home there. The interior courtyards were spacious, now filled with sight seers, like Peter, clicking cameras. The crumbling towers were the foreground to the grand view below, where Heidelberg's roofs were clustered next to the Neckar River as it flowed down the valley and away.

After an hour of inspecting the ruins, they came to the wine barrel which did indeed impress. It was so big that Mike had to climb a ladder to reach the top and Peter took his picture. Nearby in a shop there were hundreds of cards, photos and gift items to purchase.

"You can see how they discovered to make money off the tourists, Mike. Probably we should get a few cards to send back home. They'll be waiting for some news from us."

"Good idea. Can I also get a t shirt? That one with the barrel and the ruins in the background?"

"Certainly. A good way to prove you were here. How

about a souvenir for your mother?"

"I don't think she would like these beer mugs."

"Probably not. Anything for your new apartment?"

"What would that be? Something like these souvenir plates?"

"Too breakable on our trip. Look, that tapestry is lovely, put it up on the wall," Peter said as he examined a lovely woven piece that had a view of the castle.

"Very pretty. It looks like a piece of art."

"Yes, you're right. Let's get it. It's big but we can roll it up in our luggage," he said pulling out his wallet to pay.

They had a lunch of brats and sauerkraut, with a sipping cup of beer for Mike and a tall glass for Peter who asked, "How do you like the beer?"

"It's OK, I guess," said the hesitant Mike, whipping the foam from his lips.

"It's probably best if you don't tell your buddies back home about this."

Then they were off to the university student jail in the old town. It was a sobering sight with rooms filled with plain tables and chairs. Only a handful of visitors were in evidence. Notes, scribbles and graffiti of all sorts were on the walls creating a sense of disorder. Prominent black silhouettes of student heads often carried names of 19th century violators.

"Let's get out of here," said Mike, apparently not as interested or comfortable with the place as he had envisioned. Peter was reminded of the Berlin Wall with its countless social messages and drawings, many of them admittedly more inspiring than this collection. That led to their walk to the bridge, encountering on the way another passenger from the Majestic, Roger Twilling, the man they had met just briefly in Rudesheim.

"Good to see you. Recording Heidelberg, are you?" said Peter, knowing the man had been taking photos during the cruise "

"Yes, but mostly just sight-seeing. I'm a free-lancer reporter so it's fun for me to do such a gig, you could say. I'm happy to have that freedom."

"So, you're not on actual assignment? I thought you might be working for the cruise company or some advertising firm."

"No, no. Ever since Berlin, I have lots of flexibility, roaming around Europe on my own. Get to peddle my services wherever, sometimes even throwing in a cruise."

"You said Berlin. What was that?"

"Oh, a lucky strike. I was in Berlin the day the wall fell and I scribbled out lots of copy for the media. Not so much political stuff but human interest. Got really paid well and lots of recognition too, so I could call my own shots after that. Spent over a year in East Germany and Poland. Interesting. Sold lots of material."

"Germany huh? I was there about the same time." Peter paused. He didn't want to reveal his own story at this point. "So, Roger, have you got another project in the works?"

"Yes, indeed. A bit different. Going now to Bosnia and that area."

"Bosnia? Not a light caper, I would say. Just reading about it. It's still a war zone."

"Well, they say the fighting may be over soon. I hope so, but I don't plan on covering the conflict. I do better with the aftermath of violence. You know, human interest angle, like I did in Germany. Going to focus on the relief aid situation."

"What relief?"

"Mostly food, shelter for refugees. The UN and international communities are invested in Croatia and surrounding areas and so are smaller efforts like foundations and churches. But these philanthropic folks got their problems without the cover of a military or government. They have to operate often on their own. Recently their shipments got intercepted, blown up. You know, the opposition doesn't want the area stabilized so these non-profits often have to go under the radar. Need to be quiet for safely," Roger sighed.

"Quiet. What do you mean?" Peter's attention was caught. "Is there any actual aid getting through? "

"Yes, it's still working, I've been told. The donated money mysteriously still seems to be coming in, one way or another, for buying and delivering the supplies. But where, how and when? A great question. Probably through Hungary. The routes are a secret to protect the operation."

"You'd think a humanitarian effort wouldn't have to be secret." Peter frowned. "Any hint of fraud or mismanagement?"

"That's one of the points I'll going to investigate. I've got my sources."

"So now you're an investigator, finding the money trail," Peter said with a hint of amusement.

"Yes, a journalist should also always look for the facts, no matter what."

They parted and walked on. As it was sunny with only a threat of clouds on the horizon, many strollers were out and about on the walkway. After a bit, they paused and turned around to see the old city and again were taken by the panorama of the historic buildings, the castle looming above and the surrounding wooded hills.

"Years ago, the philosophers saw this same scene, with the exception of the crowds," said Peter. "It does lend itself to contemplation."

Mike pulled out his sketch pad and pencil from his

backpack and started to draw. He seemed to be already half way through the tablet. This activity enabled Peter some quiet moments as he leaned against the stone railing, folding his hands across his body. He thought about his own days as a college teacher.

What would retirement be like when he returned? Perhaps time to reflect and access his life? He didn't have a bridge but he did have his back yard fully accessorized with outdoor furniture, a fire pit, Margie's flowers and abundance of towering trees. It was a great Illinois setting, especially when the mosquitos weren't swarming, he acknowledged.

An elderly lady passed by, and noticing the boy at work, smiled her approval and nodded at Peter. A sudden pang of homesickness filled him. He saw Margie and the girls in his mind, wishing they were here to experience that subtle moment. He was happy to feel their strong essence so far from home.

Once back on the bus, they were speedily returned through the night to the Majestic which was now anchored at Wurzburg, having continued on to the river Main after leaving the Rhine. The cruise patrons had already had a city tour the previous day, only allowing for an individual quick visit before the river journey continued toward Bamberg. The Baroque and Rococo richly decorated harbor was impressive but Peter suggested they skip the visit because they were too tired from their late night to venture out. However, a museum containing the famous wooden sculpture of Adam and Eve by Tilman Riemenschneider was one thing he would have appreciated seeing.

Mike wasn't disappointed and immediately headed for the dining room. Peter however, had knowledge of the city to compensate for their cancelation. It had it's beginning in the 7th century. Oddly it was a Celtic missionary, St. Kilian, who had come to convert them to Christianity and it was their tribesmen that built the massive fortress, *Marienberg*, still standing on the steep banks of the River Main. It was used as a stronghold for hundreds of years. In modern times, Wurzburg had suffered extreme damage in the war, destroying almost all of the churches and especially damaging the *Residenz*. Extensive restoration had taken years to finish but now it blended easily into the long history of Wurzburg.

Years ago, when Margie and he had taken the family on their first visit to Germany, they had included Wurzburg in their travels, trying to engulf as many sights as they could. The girls were still very young and were already tired of seeing yet another church, and another museum and another palace. When they came to the Bishop's *Residenz*, they were not in the best mood and were squirming about, waiting for the tour to begin, even as workmen nearby were carefully laying out replacement parquet floors.

He remembered them running up the glorious Grand Staircase ahead of the serious tour guide, an older woman with thick spectacles. She was of stout frame and voice, who quickly brought them to attention with a sharp tap of her walking stick.

Her oral rebuke was something like "What can one expect from those rambunctious and obnoxious American offspring?" Resentment probably still lingered with her toward the Allied air raids that had destroyed so much of the city. However, after that remark, there was no way that his family could enjoy seeing the world's greatest ceiling painting by Tiepolo, the greatest Baroque building in Germany designed by Balthasar Newman, or the lovely *Gartensaal* with the blooming flowers beyond.

"We probably should have skipped seeing the *Residenz* on that visit too," he said to himself.

The journey continued, offering the guests some relaxation time on deck to enjoy the splendid views of the countryside with small towns and beautiful vineyards, the largest wine growing area in Germany. Here the river diminished but deep diggings had enlarged the waterway's depth to afford cruise ships to navigate. However, a summer rain shower engulfed them later, sending them down just in time for lunch of oxtail soup and potato dumplings.

A dancing program was planned for the afternoon and Julie was quick to reach Peter in hopes of luring him to participate but he skillfully said he had paper work to do and dodged the bullet. Too bad Margie wasn't here. He missed her, her teasing smile, her clear blue eyes and flowing brown hair swept back. Holding her close. They had often enjoyed dancing through the years.

"Oh, all right then. Come along children, let's see what this is all about," Julie said, pulling the youngsters along. Mike followed but gave Peter a deep scowl in passing. He probably had not had much experience in that kind of activity.

Later when he returned, Peter had finished his favorite crime novel and shuffled through his crate of photos, still not recognizing many faces. Shaking his head thinking time does go on and images of the past just did that – passed on.

"So, how was it?" he said to Mike. The boy smiled. "I didn't have to dance, just the older folks. Kari didn't want to either so we just talked and laughed. But that Aunt Julie hitched up with several partners and seemed to have a ball. She really gets around."

"Well then, it turned out OK, right? And tomorrow we'll be in Bamberg. I'll get to see my old friend Klaus. He was my buddy when I was your age."

With that, they got ready for bed while the rain softly pattered on the window.

BAMBERG

UPON ARRIVING IN Bamberg, one of Germany's most historical cities, they were immediately met by Klaus who was going to give them his own city tour. He was a big man, balding with a smart clipped moustache and rimless glasses with shining blue eyes. He wore casual clothes but his manner definitely mirrored his occupation as a business man, now retired, but having run a successful transportation company.

Mike sensed the ease the men had with each another even though they hadn't seen one another very often in the many years since the war. He had heard about their friendship as boys in Dusseldorf but he couldn't quite imagine that connection from this meeting as Klaus gave him a very strong adult hand shake in greeting.

"Let's see the city first, then we'll stop by my place," he said. "I know you have to be back on the ship tonight." Obviously proud of the city, he started his dialogue with quick historical references, like Bamberg celebrating its 1,000 years in 1973 and being a World Heritage Center. It contained two thousand historical buildings. Culture wise, it published the first book in German and had a rich musical heritage, the present symphony being world renowned. Peter thought his information was mostly for Mike's sake, but he appreciated it also as he had never been in Bamberg before. Klaus, however, had lived there for many years.

Built on seven hills, the exterior zones of the city were rather mundane, having a busy commercial life and Klaus pointed out his former warehouse complex rather casually in passing, saying that there wasn't anything noteworthy for a tourist to see. But his voice grew stronger as they neared the center and they certainly saw the reason for his enthusiasm. The old *Burgerstadt* was filled with picturesque structures and a market square which had milling people, even soldiers in American uniforms, scattered among the throng. The stands displayed every sort of fruit, vegetables, bread, household items and electronics.

They stopped at one to sample and buy some pretzels as they wandered up the pedestrian street to where the River Regnitz flowed. A large modern statue by Mitori seemed to challenge the onlookers with its location and rotund shape. A group of young men were paddling kayaks in the stream below and young women were shouting to them from the bridge. Directly below on either side were dwellings that once were fishermen's homes, now shops and galleries, causing it to be called little Venice. Then came the old town hall, Bamberg's famous landmark, built on a small island in the middle of the river.

"Hey, Mike, look at that," said Peter, obviously impressed.

The building was a mixture of styles, with sections cantilevered over the water. Part of it looked rustic with half timbered walls and part was Rococo with a fading mural on the side. Klaus pointed out an interesting visual trick on the wall where a section showed an artist holding his paint brushes while his leg extended out in space from the one-dimensional painting.

The river separated two historical sections of the city.

Crossing it where a sculpture of Queen *Kunigunda* stood, they climbed up the surrounding slope to be in the ecclesiastical area, *Bishopsstadt,* dominated by the *Kaiserdom,* or cathedral, with its four tall towers. Mike liked the heavy doors, having decorative iron hinges and surrounded by stone pillars with religious figures carved into the recesses. In the distance was an Abbey, also a splendid structure, carrying his name, *Michaelsberg.*

Inside the *Dom,* which had Romanesque and early Gothic elements, tourists were gathered around to see one of Germany's most famous symbols of medieval life and also the symbol of the city, the *Bamberger Reiter.* The grey stone sculpture overlooking the sanctuary high up on a wall was of a life-sized man on horseback wearing a crown over his unusual straight chin length hair. Otherwise, he didn't carry any weapons or sport any other decorations.

Mike raised himself on his toes for a better view. "So, what's the deal with this guy?" he asked.

"He's very old and mysterious. No one knows why or who made it," said Peter. Mike took that as a hint and pulled out his sketch pad and drew a quick drawing.

Klaus added that the church was organized in 1,002 AD, but the sculpture probably was completed around 1,237 AD when the present building was dedicated. It is the oldest equestrian sculpture made since classical antiquity but much speculation had been voiced over the years to whom it was to represent. Some thought it was King Henry, perhaps an important knight, a saint or some type of messiah.

"Even the Nazis claimed it was a symbol of chivalry and they said that Graf von Stauffenberg was inspired by it in his quest to assassinate Hitler. So, take your pick," laughed Klaus.

Outside they wandered to the beautiful garden of the

Bishop residence, lined with trees and 4,500 roses. The balconies were also laden with geranium baskets. Peter took photos and Mike with his ever-ready sketch book, drew the towers. This led them to a break and they headed down to the commercial street where another famous feature of Bamberg awaited them – a restaurant that featured smoked beer. They ordered food too and both Mike and Peter selected the specialty, Bamberg Onion, which had baked ground pork and bacon with gravy resting inside a big onion shell and served with mashed potatoes.

"Want to have a sip of this beer?" asked Peter cautiously but Mike hesitated.

"Oh, that's Ok," said Klaus. "It's not to everyone's liking. Smoked beer is an acquired taste." Peter silently agreed.

The historical tour and the good meal made Mike sleepy and he soon slouched down in his chair and dozed off while the men kept talking in German and drinking. Their conversation turned to the past in Dusseldorf where they had lived near one another growing up and both were part of the troupe of youngsters that had been taken to Hungary for protection during the war.

"So, Klaus, when did you actually move to Bamberg?"

"A few years after you left, now almost forty years ago. When I came back from America, you know from the prisoner of war camp in Louisiana, we were detained in France for nine more months before we were released. I spent more time as a prisoner than a soldier, having been drafted as a sixteen-year-old kid four months before the end. We had emergency training and guarded a munitions dump, only to get captured a week later," he sighed.

"Being younger than you, I was lucky to miss that horror but life after the war was no picnic either, you remember. I was happy to go to Chicago."

"You had luck, that's for sure. But when I returned, I was eighteen, no more schooling, no work, little food, few prospects. As you knew, Dusseldorf was still sweeping up the debris. But I got a job driving a truck with a moving company down here in Bavaria, so I took it. It led me into that business and I stayed here ever since. Glad of it. Proud of this place."

"You certainly did well for yourself, from truck driver to owner of the company, a big company at that." Peter shifted in his chair, trying to move to pleasurable memories "Remember the good times before the war when we played football at the old church yard? How Pastor Lend yelled at us for ruining the grass?"

"Yah, good times," said Klaus but he couldn't help himself. "But later the fires scorched that grass and burned the whole damn church down with him in it."

"Terrible times."

"Oh, God yes. You know that's something they didn't know much about in the states. Bombs and fires. They didn't know much about our football either. They called it soccer. At the camp we were allowed recreation every day, so we chased that ball around, reviving us, even after being dead tired from a muggy day of picking sugar cane. And it could be really hot and we picked lots of cane, I can tell you."

"We got to play football when we were in Hungary too, remember?

"Yah, that was pretty good fun, especially for little kids far from home. We were lucky that we didn't have to do more chores," said Klaus, obviously comparing that to his later experience in the prisoner of war camp.

"There was some advantage at the time being in Hungary, of being student guests sponsored by the German government."

Peter also thought of his other less than desirable time later as a city boy in his country experience.

They both sat silently for a moment as wistful memories of the time floated into Peter's mind. He heard the punch of the ball, the huffing of the boys' exertion in the game, their laughter as they played on the grassy yard behind the encampment of tents where they studied and slept. He saw the nearby large manor house of the estate with its covered porches where they ate their meals, the orchard surrounding it, the well where they drew their water for the day.

He heard the workmen talking in the barns, the noise of horses being harnessed, the mooing of the cows waiting for their feed. Beyond lay the modest houses of the estate's workers, the fenced sheep pasture, the productive fields in the lower valley, the vineyards on the southern side of the rolling hills.

"But they certainly used us with the tramping of the grapes," said Klaus.

"I thought my feet would stay purple forever," laughed Peter."

He knew the sentimental picture of that bucolic life on the estate, actually a remnant of Austrian-Hungarian times, didn't stay that way long after the boys left when the invasion of Soviet troops changed everything. When war ended, the master of the house, Herr Redmann, had gone to Budapest, representing that area in government talks, trying to avoid turning it into a captured communistic state. The vast ethnic German land holding owners were seen as a threat and their lands confiscated. Stalin was cleansing the whole Balkan and Ukraine area of them, sending them to Siberia, even if they had lived there for over a hundred years.

When Herr Redmann returned, he found his home burned,

his estate divided, his wife and children never found, apparently killed according to local rumor. Peter would later learn more about his astonishing journey when he fled to Germany as a refugee, being in Dresden the night of the Allied fire-bombing of the city and jumping into the Elbe River to escape the flames. Amazingly, he later immigrated to the United States as an older man, landing in Detroit where Peter had been able to visit him. So far removed from his aristocratic background, he'd became an enthusiastic American citizen who worked as a craftsman in a motor building plant where he labored until his retirement.

"How was the camp in America?" Peter asked Klaus.

"Actually, in perspective, not too bad, nothing like in France where we were held before being released. We worked like dogs fixing railroad tracks and tunnels and we never had enough to eat. The Americans fed us well in their camp, knowing we needed energy to work. Somehow the Europeans never got that concept dealing with their prisoners. And as I was the youngest, they treated me rather special, I believe. Sorry for me, I guess, but the security was pretty loose and they sometimes gave me time out. I can say that for them."

"So, you found some Americans good human beings?" Peter asked, a little in jest.

"Yes, that's right and even in Bamberg we have quite a history with them. The Allied barracks have been here for so long, they are part of the scene. West Germany was occupied but also protected from the East for years by those US forces."

"It's just like in Heidelberg," said Peter. "I imagine there were also financial benefits to the city as well as some cultural influences."

"It certainly helped me. Most of my business was moving their families in and out. My limited English even got better. It

will be a slim day around here when they close up this instil-
lation. However, I'm glad to be retired. How about you?"

They agreed and each ordered another beer. The waitress
kept their count with a mark her pencil made on the beer
coasters. She smiled at Mike, now limp in the chair. "Does he
want anything?" she said.

"I doubt it. He's out. Good food and too many churches."

"So, how's your family?" asked Klaus.

"Doing passable, I think. The girls are all grown up and
having some troubles of their own. The typical stuff, you
know, but Margie has her hands full caring for her mother
who is with us at the moment." He didn't want to elaborate.

"Yah, that can be tough. I only had a little of that, being
my sister lived closer and cared for my mother and I'd lost
my father on the Russia front. Like you, I never had much of
a father but I never got married either, so no problems there."

"Tell me, Klaus, never any women in your life?"

"I did fancy a few. Especially one that married someone
else after I got home. Actually, after the war young men were
scare so there were good pickings but nothing that stuck, you
could say. Now I'm too old."

They laughed at that and their conversation rambled on to
Bavarian politics and international issues, becoming slurred
with the introduction of a few more beers. They got more pencil marks on their coasters. Then suddenly they realized the
time slipping away and they roused Mike.

"My apartment isn't far. Let's take a walk."

A mighty ring of church bells echoed when they left the
restaurant. The sounds so typical of Europe. As they ambled,
Mike kept seeing niches in the walls of the stucco buildings displaying many religious figures. Exterior architecture
here had to remain historic but interior spaces were often

renovated. Klaus' home was in such a traditional building but his large second story abode was very modern.

It was quit beautifully furnished for a bachelor businessman, with stylish modern Scandinavian style furniture, green house plants and a fancy balcony to make up for no other outdoor space. A circular fireplace with two enormous cats resting nearby was the focal point. He served coffee and had sweet treats in glass nut dishes in his very slimmed lined kitchen and he proudly showed off his newly installed bathroom which looked like a vision from a fancy hotel suite or spa. An office and three bedrooms, swimming in luxurious touches, completed the tour.

It was very spacious, not bursting at the seams with family everywhere like in his home in Illinois, thought Peter, but he didn't care for the neutral color scheme and shinning surfaces. For him it was rather cold and impersonal but he knew the style was considered very chic so he was careful to properly praise the décor to his successful friend. Modern Germans had certainly earned their right for distinctive taste.

Klaus gave them a quick ride back to the Majestic, now docked at the Main Danube canal, and he wished them well with a slight tremor in his voice. It was obviously hard for both men to say goodbye because their comfortable present day was still shadowed by their past. Along the walkway they saw people mingling, some of whom were the cruise passengers back from their city tour who were getting ready to board. Out of the crowd came Emma, waving to them to hurry along.

"Let's get going," Peter shouted to Mike who had been lingering behind, looking at the bridge which had a vast collection of pad locks clamped on its framework. These were symbols of lovers or friends locked in devotion to each other with names and dates painted on them. The owners threw away the keys in the river. Mike wondered if he would ever do such a thing.

Just then a gang of teenagers burst from the crowd, deliberately bumping into Emma, unsuccessfully grabbing at her back pack and knocking her to the ground. But one of them did get her tote bag as she fell and with a noisy approval, they ran off toward a nearby alley. Immediately Peter rushed toward Emma, offering assistance, but Mike's eyes followed the gang. Before they disappeared, he saw them tossing out the contents of the tote, probably the maps and itinerary sheets of paper that Emma carried. They obviously didn't find what they were looking for, but incensed, Mike followed them. Further down the street, he spied the tote which obviously also had been tossed away.

He grabbed it and picked up some of the maps on his way back to dock side. There Peter and another man were assisting Emma into the ship and he hurried up to join them. Seeing Mike, Peter said, "We're getting her to the first aid station down below. I'll meet you back at our cabin."

When Peter returned, he seemed flustered. "She'll be ok, just a few bruises. Her shoulder hurts. But it was such a stupid thing."

"I'm sure they were looking for money."

"And they got away. I imagine no way to track them."

"But Gramps, I picked up the tote bag, also some of her maps. Here they are."

They examined the bag, no worse for wear, but something about it, peaked Peter's interest after they took out the maps that Mike had gathered. "It seems heavy, doesn't it?" He shook it, and turned it upside down, then he inspected it again.

"You know, it's one of those bags that has a secret pocket here at the bottom. Just like those sandwich bags that seal things up."

"They use that to put in wet swim suits and stuff like that at the beach," said Mike, feeling better informed. But no swim suits emerged. Instead, they saw rolls of Euros as they pulled it open. "My God, it's money. The gang really missed out."

"And lots of money. Actually, hundreds wrapped up," gasped Peter, immediately visualizing scenes of mafia dealings in movies that he'd seen. It made him breathless. "We have to get this back to Emma now. It's hers. She'll have some explanation, I'm sure. Wait here, I'll be back." He said as he abruptly left with the tote bag.

Mike looked over the maps. She might want them too but some were smudged from the grimy street. He could get them to her later, he thought, but one was pretty dirty. He opened it up and noticed an ink ring marked around a street he recognized near the *Dom*. He hadn't seen her but she would have taken the city tour group there, he knew, and thinking nothing more of it, tossed it into the waste basket.

When Peter returned, he said he had found Emma back in her cabin, resting.

"So, what's the deal? About the money?" inquired Mike immediately.

"A little strange. She was upset, understandably, after the assault on the street. But quite surprised about the tote, thanking me profusely. I told her about seeing the money and then she became very quiet for a bit."

"So, what's the deal with the money? Did she say?" Mike was getting impatient.

Peter explained her response. "She carries the money for a non-profit group offering assistance in Croatia. She explained her sympathies for the cause because she had been born in the area. Her parents moved to Holland when she was small but had always retained a close connection to that culture. Various sympathizers in western Europe meet her at appointed places and contribute goodly sums to be delivered in Budapest for relief projects."

"Isn't that rather dangerous?"

"Yes, I'd think so but I didn't say anything to her. It's her business and her money."

It was the same story about charities that Roger Twilling had told Peter in Heidelberg and it seemed believable. Anyway, he believed her. "She begged me to keep it a secret as the operation would suffer and she could be in danger if some factions would know about it. She also might lose her job if that were known."

"That teen gang thing was just an accident then?"

"I think so. But we'll keep it quiet. You'll have to go along with me on this, Buddy. Keep it to ourselves. Ok?"

"Yah, sure, Gramps. My word."

That seemed to solve the issue and they settled down for the next stretch of the journey which continued now on the Main Danube Canal. The building of this long waterway connected western Europe to the Danube and enabled shipping all the way to the Black Sea. The first stop would be Nuremburg and the information sheet slipped under the door describing the upcoming events and sights gave them more information.

The water route had been a dream since Charlemagne with unsuccessful attempts to build it through many years. Even Crazy King Ludwig tried but only in recent times did it get completed. Seen as a commercial dream for transporting goods like grain, steel and fertilizer, it now also afforded tourist vessels great access to cross continental travel. The canal itself was 100 miles long with 15 locks opening up 2,200 miles of navigation through 15 countries.

"It says it changed the landscape and affected some of the eco system but it's one of Europe's greatest achievements. As important as the Panama Canal, I would say," said Peter.

Soon they felt a slowing of the boat's momentum, then a stopping. They were entering a lock and Mike jumped up, dashing to the door and out to the deck. He wanted to see what was happening. Peter followed, camera in hand. The engines were still idling but they could see large gates closing behind, sealing the vessel in a box some forty feet wide with high cement walls surrounding it.

With a noisy entering rush of water, the Majestic began to rise. A man at the front secured ropes to an anchor on the wall which rose with the water level and also stabilized the vessel. After nearly a half hour and a hundred feet, they were near the top of the lock. Then the ropes were released and the forward gates engaged, opening to the same high-water level beyond. The engines suddenly roared, sending the ship forward to the man-made channel ahead. Like the whole journey, it required careful navigation.

"It's like climbing a stairway," said the astonished Mike to Kari who had joined him to watch the action.

"We are to climb all the way to Nuremberg," she said smugly. "Quite exciting."

He retrieved his sketch pad and started to draw. Peter took his picture. Mike came up with a walled watery looking border but soon focused on the girl in the middle, head held high, who was posing perfectly still for the artist.

NUREMBERG

GOING THROUGH MORE locks, they arrived at Nuremberg. The water route generally gained height and at one point near the city, they saw a roadway actually going under the artificial canal. Peter had some idea of the place, mostly known as a toy manufacturing center, and also the makers of Christmas treats, like *marzipan* and *lebkuchen*. But obviously there wouldn't be any *Christkindelsmarkt* in the summertime.

Stopping to eat, they ordered a tasty dish of breaded carp cooked in vinegar with dill sauce, oddly a local specialty as fish were raised commercially in the area's ponds. However, any satisfactory thoughts of sweets and scrumptious meals soon disappeared as they started on a special city tour, featuring the other famous feature of Nuremberg – the historical sites of the Nazi regime.

"I know this Nazi stuff might be a bit boring for you, Mike, but I think you should learn about this part of history."

"It's Ok, Gramps. I've seen lots of war movies."

"Well, good then, but realize that these places were the real thing, not movie sets. Hitler had his big rallies here, spreading Nazi propaganda and lies to the nation. It was actually the cause of all the horror that came later," he said.

It reminded Peter about the tidal wave of Hollywood films

centered on the war, many of which he disliked. An early TV series, "The Rat Patrol", had been one that was satisfactory for him. In it the actor, Austrian native Hans Gudegast, was a favorite even when he later changed his name to Eric Braden and became famous as Victor in the "Young and Restless" daytime drama.

The very large Zeppelin field, named for the Count who developed the dirigible, lay before them. As large as twelve football fields, it was a place of past parades and huge political Nazi demonstrations and now an occasional open-air rock concert. At the moment it was very quiet with only a few people strolling about and some boys playing football. Beyond that rose the large concrete stadium, designed by Albert Speer. The whole area could hold 400,000 people at a time. Even fenced off, he felt stunned and recognized it immediately for he had seen it in movie clips when young, as well as later on American documentary programs about the war.

Raising his eyes above to the sky, he envisioned Hitler's airplane as he landed for a rally here in the famous propaganda movie, "Triumph of the Will", by Leni Riefenstahl. Thousands of people had been in attendance in the stadium and it was later seen by everyone throughout the country in dark movie houses. Without a doubt, the rallies were a tremendous show of power for his government.

He shivered, still with that remembrance of long ago. How could a charismatic leader influence a nation to follow him into such chaos? With his ideas of superiority and dominance, Hitler led them and so many others to disaster in the end. Here was this very place, where chants rose in the air and tens of thousands of people stood in orderly rows and waved their flags in mass obedience.

Now long removed from being a child, Peter stood still, looking at the scene with anger in his veins. The slogans of survivors came to him. Let us never forget, he thought. Don't let it ever happen again.

"So, what are you thinking?" said Mike, noticing his grandfather's stern face.

"They obviously got rid of the big swastika sign that towered over the stadium but I'm wondering why they haven't blown up the whole damn thing."

"Probably because it's so big. Like a big, big football arena at home."

"Look out there, that entire field was filled with people and soldiers as well as the grandstand here. The *Reich* or empire was meant to last a thousand years. Such power, such arrogance."

"You didn't like them, did you?"

"That's right, but I was in a small way part of it all."

"How did they get such power?"

"Great question and no decent answer. In olden days, men fought for land and one of them became the leader, then he got power hungry and became king with absolute authority. Later his descendants just inherited that power of the throne and subjects were ruled because of tradition."

"But what happened?"

"After time, many monarchs fell. There was an opening for some other type of government. Democracies, republics, social states that became communistic states. Some worked, some didn't. Leaders took over again, usually with propaganda and good organization, gaining a following, and then came force with absolute control. In Germany we got authoritative rule like that, you know, led by one man and his significant group. It's called fascism, tyranny."

Mike was trying to follow. "Then came the war, righ

"Earlier one war got rid of the monarch and it took ᴜ other to get rid of Hitler, the *Fuhrer*. Looking at this place, let's hope we've learned a lesson," said Peter, deep in thought. Perhaps after all, it was warranted to keep these places visible to remind people about the mistakes of the past. However, he worried that in Mike's generation there would be a problem. They couldn't forget an experience they'd never had; they might not be able to learn a lesson from this place of history

They entered the tour bus which took them to the impressive U-shaped building, the Nazi Congress Hall, surrounded by a lake, which was also part of the four-square mile complex. It was made with polished granite but never entirely finished or used at the time but now some sections were occupied by various civic organizations.

"Gosh, it looks like the Coliseum in Rome," said Mike.

"That's right. Only it's bigger. Designed to impress." He huffed. Peter could have gone on but he stood silently. "I've seen enough. Let's wait in the bus until the others are finished."

The bus pulled to the next attraction, the Palace of Justice, the site of the War Crimes Tribunal in 1946 where the Allies tried 22 major Nazi criminals. The chamber 600 looked like a traditional courtroom but Peter could feel the cold history in the air of that room. When it was all over 12 men were sentenced to death. Leaders like Hitler, Goebels, Goring and Himmler had already committed suicide. Another 185 leaders were tried later.

Another optional tour was a visit to the underground bunkers and tunnels which had safely housed art pieces during the war. One of his favorite stories was about the Monument Men of the US Army who were actual art historians and saved countless works from destruction there as the tumult raged over them.

However, Mike was getting weary with the visit. So, Peter said, "Enough of this history. Let's go see something else."

The bus drove by the ancient wall, a hospital built in 1332 which had housed lepers, several castles and got to the main square where a market was going on. The *Frauen* Church and a large fountain gave it the typical German setting. The guide stressed the beauty of the spot, especially at night when this and other buildings were lit up all over the city.

"That's another thing I remember seeing in the film," said Peter, still mulling his past. "The Nazis really lit up those rally fields at night with search lights into the sky. In those days, that was something of a technical wonder."

Mike, not connecting to that, came up with a question. "Which river is this?"

"The Pegnitz. Can be confused with the Regnitz in Bamberg."

"Hard up for names, I guess," said Mike.

Peter thought to himself that Mike was getting more curious and perceptive as the trip went along. He was indeed a good companion for his age and his drawings really showed talent. "You should like the Durer house. An important artist. We're going to see that next."

Albrecht Durer became famous in the 16th century for his contribution to the Golden Age of the Renaissance. As a northern artist, he excelled in woodcuts and engravings. The family, originally from Hungary, had settled in Nuremberg and their upper wood timbered house, where Durer lived and worked, still stood on a striking corner of the old town. It now housed a museum with examples of his work and demonstrations of the engraving and printing techniques Durer used at the time.

Peter thought this would interest his grandson and Mike did seem absorbed. They browsed the many prints available for sale. Many of them were religious themed and very complex, revealing even to a casual observer the challenging form of the engraver's art. Peter settled on the famous one of Praying Hands as a present for Margie. She could use heavenly help, he knew.

Mike, however, found another series featuring animals which drew his attention. The Rhinoceros, a daunting piece which was clad in armor-like skin and heavy features gave the viewer as sense of the strength of the beast, if not an accurate portrayal. He then came across the Young Hare, a touching realistic print and immediately loved it. They bought these favorite pieces and then left.

Back on the ship, they were soon raising again higher through the many locks of the canal, getting to 1400 feet above sea level. That was because the Franconian Jura mountain range lay in route to Passau. Since this took a long time with limited views going up and down, the ship's sitting rooms became popular places for the passengers to pass the time. They offered comfortable chairs, board games, puzzles and small libraries.

At their deck's nearby room, Peter settled down with a local newspaper filled with the latest news about the Bosnian War while Mike and Kari played monopoly. Julie whizzed by, took in the quiet scene, and hastily went off to hunt in the ship's gift shop. She also wanted to make another stop at the lounge for an early drink of her favorite red wine.

The news interested Peter for a while but then he closed the paper and rested his eyes. The movement of the boat seemed to usher him into thoughts long lay hidden. It didn't take long before he was lost again in his own past which he had so often dismissed in his busy life in America.

He saw again his gentle mother, Erma, going to work at the post office in order to provide for the fatherless family. Her curly auburn hair sticking out of her hat and her well-worn red woolen coat made a colorful image as she trudged down the grey street. She was lucky to have that position because most able-bodied men were gone. Tired, she had long silences when she returned. Always her quietness, her distance seemed like there was something else on her mind.

The smoke rings from her cigarette, usually bought on the black market, would rise like her thoughts into the air. She also had a stoic explanation about the cancer that was growing in her body. The opium treatment pushed her speech and spirit farther away even when she temporarily improved. Later when she was at death's door, they said she seemed so willing to go.

Then Peter shifted in his chair, his startled eyes opening wide because his grandmother's visage appeared. Her tending to the home and hungry children was a blessing and a curse for them. With zealous religious guidance and stern character, she fed them but harshly controlled them by language and physical abuse. Her walking stick was a dangerous tool, often hitting its mark on their behinds and arms. He remembered her mutterings and hasty walks, be it to the damaged church or the ration station. The bombs increased her paranoia and she suspected all and everyone of misdeeds. The children became a testing ground for hysterical outbursts of injustice as they were being rushed to the cellar for safety. The memory of her was a wound healed over but a nasty scare remained.

No mark of such remembrance came to him about his father. There was only mystery, quiet whisperings. His father had simply evaporated from their lives. As a boy he felt an emptiness but not a defined loss. Sorrow didn't overwhelm him, just a questioning that was never answered. Even now the vague identification of the photos in the crate hadn't stirred much recognition.

But the question of the crate and its contents did remind him. He couldn't take all of that back home so he had to make a decision about what to do with it. Mike and Kari seemed occupied so he went to the cabin to sort out the materials. He hadn't actually gone through most of it so it was a good time to do it more thoroughly.

He began with the photo album which was familiar. It contained the family collection, starting with his parents wedding photo and then various examples of the sisters and him during their baby and early childhood years. But the remaining black pages of the album were empty, like family life had ended there. Yes, that's when the father vanished and war came. He could easily pick out the photos because they weren't sealed to the page, only held in place with cornered paper brackets. He wanted to keep these but could dispose of the album because it would take up too much room in his luggage.

Next came a small cookie tin, which he had opened before, containing many loose photos that he recognized and had dates or identification written on the backs. Some were of the young grandchildren, both those of his sisters' kids in Hamburg and ones he had sent her. There were three taken of his mother as a young woman wearing fancy clothes, obviously during the roaring twenties, possibly at Carnival. She was lovely with a wide smile and glowing eyes, but he found her more familiar with two other photos done when she was older. And there was the early photo of his father that he'd had trouble recognizing before when they were in Dusseldorf.

On the bottom of the tin was a sealed envelope which he opened. It contained many photos, most centering on a similar group of men. He could identify his father in the midst of them, some taken in a pub with smiling faces, holding up steins in celebration. There was one that was in a bowling alley, perhaps part of the *kegle club,* many smiling. Another one looked like a chorus group with people wearing choir gowns but his father was in a tuxedo standing in front. He was obviously a singer of some note. A moment in time at a concert. All were glimpses of his early life, unknown to his son.

Then came a straight photo of his father, carrying a brief case and wearing a suit with tie and hat. It must have been a business shot. Others were three photos of men sitting around a table but it was a serious scene. Peter looked more closely at it. His father was holding a pen, some were smoking and others were reading notes. There were newspapers on the table, a number of other sheets of paper and something that looked like a poster. He couldn't make out the writing on them. He knew this wasn't a social gathering - it was a meeting.

Another photo showed the similar set up but one of the men was wearing a priest collar. It caught his attention and then he knew. It was his father's brother, Father Wilhelm. His mother had spoken of him so he did know that his priest uncle had opposed the Nazis, spoken against them even in church and was later given house arrest along with some other priests. People wondered what happened but none of them were ever seen again.

The other tragedy of his father's family was with the youngest son, Fritz, who had been drafted late into the army and was sent to the Eastern front. He never returned either so the Hartman family lost all three of their sons. They lived in the same area as Peter but the boy saw little of them during the war, either because of some indifference or perhaps their disapproval. Everyone at that time needed to survive on their own terms.

The priest in the photo, however, was part of this earlier meeting and that likely made Peter's father and the group some type of political activists. They weren't communists he was sure, but certainly they were anti-Nazi. His mother must have known his activity by keeping the photos stashed away, perhaps hiding evidence, but not wanting to entirely erase a remembrance of him.

Suddenly Herman Hartman became more alive to him. This was a small trail of information that he never knew anything about but it could be believed. The man had indeed been involved in something organized, something possibly dangerous during those years. Yes, he would save all of these photos.

"Hey, Gramps, what are you doing?"

Startled, Peter saw Mike and Kari in the doorway. He responded, "Going through stuff. What are you doing? I thought you were still doing games."

"No, we're off to the ballroom for a concert. They have a band playing," he said. Then looking at the pile of photos, he added, "Why don't you make a copy of them all? Minimize if you have to. Mom would like them, I'm sure."

"Good idea."

"They must have a copy machine on board."

"You're full of info. Thanks."

With that the kids were off and Peter packed his bundle together and set off for the office. He did find a copy machine which he was free to use and then headed back to his room, only to realize the added amount of material he now had. And he'd have to label them so they would know what they were looking at. What were they looking at, those elusive unknown pictures of the past?

Now came the books. He needed to glean the assortment, some of which he recognized from his youth. They must have meant something to his mother so he started a saved stack. A worn book of poetry, a keeper. A not so worn old Goethe edition. A keeper. A small leather-bound Bible slid between several volumes. Still another keeper. At the bottom even came a used cook book, which Margie might like, but it was in German, of course, and in metric measurements so it wouldn't be very useful.

The exercise baffled him. He was getting nowhere. He'd just have to go through everything again. He started with the cook book. Yes, that could go. How about Goethe? He was a German professor, after all, and should value an old edition but he had recent copies of his works at home. That can go. His mother's historical novels could go.

He was getting somewhere when he picked up the small Bible. It was small and in fair shape; it couldn't be his grandmother's, which he would gladly toss. He flipped open the cover and saw a long list of names which he recognized in his mother's handwriting. It contained good family birth records which he'd value. Several religious book marks and funeral notices of friends fell out of the Bible, also a folded clipping yellowed with age.

Opening it up, some onion-thin flower petals fell out into his lap. Touching them, they crumbled into mere slivers and he stopped. They had to be some romantic or significant filmy message from the past. His distant mother must have had such emotional times, of course, even if he hadn't known her in that way.

Reading the old clipping, almost as delicate as the petals,

he saw it was an official notice, complete with a swastika stamp on top, from the office of the Rhine River Patrol.

It contained startling information, totally unknown to Peter. The frozen remains of Herman Hartman had been found on March 10,1939 and identified by his engraved pocket watch, along the Rhine River banks, mile marker indicated. Cause of death - assumed drowning. Date of death - unknown Notice to nearest relative – unknown.

Somehow, they must have found her and she possessed this certificate. She'd never mentioned anything about it to them, even after the war when they were older. But now sitting in his cabin on the cruise ship, Majestic, Peter learned of his father's death more than fifty years later. He felt numb by the information, even as tears flowed down his cheeks. Images overwhelmed him. The blackness of the frozen corpse, the stiff cloth remnants clinging to the body, the matted hair full of dirt and weeds. So that, he realized, was what happened.

Peter did suddenly remember a strange evening when his mother sat quietly crying. This must have been the time she got the news. Her husband had been gone for months with no word, possibly abandoning the family, some thought. This had answered a question of what, where and how for her but probably not why. Peter's older sister, old enough to hear and understand things, had said people whispered that he was killed by the regime and some said he killed himself. Peter, being too young, hadn't understood.

However, it wasn't so unusual, he now knew. Besides the war itself, it was a time when people often were killed or disappeared, especially if they were Jews or Gypsies or those with disabilities. But Herman Hartman wasn't one of them. Did his father really fit into the other dangerous category, the political enemies of Hitler?

Peter looked out at the landscape, now coming into view as the ship rose in the lock. It seemed like something was coming into view, something long in the shadows, now rising up into the light. Clearly some weight was being lifted off of him but he wasn't to the top of the lock, to complete knowledge yet. How he died, yes, drowning in a river, but exactly why he died in the river. Many possibilities. Thrown or pushed into the river? Could it have been simply an accident or some argument with an angry acquaintance? Herman the activist, possibly killed because of his political ideas? Or his own wish, jumping off a bridge in deep despair?

Questions kept developing in his mind. Why? Had his mother and grandmother known the details? Why was the story silenced? In those years, there were things people just didn't talk about. Suicide was a sin, punished by going to hell and political opposition was likewise a deal with death. Both options held great shame or danger to one's family. No private investigations, no matter how just, were possible. Just be silent and say nothing.

Obviously, his fearful mother had escaped into silence for safety but his grandmother certainly didn't react quietly to other factors in life. She was angry and blamed all and everyone for everything in a torrent of fear and anxiety. Even her Catholic faith became an extreme exercise, forcibly making the children into constant obedience and excessive church attendance. The children pleaded with their mother about the crazy grandmother's treatment but the response was always the same. She was needed.

"But you can escape, we can't," Peter remembered saying. He was scolded for that outburst but the words might have hit close to the truth. She probably was happy to get away from the tension of the house at times. He realized now that their grandmother's furry might have come from her resentment of the situation and the responsibility thrust on her. But after being bombed out in her own apartment, she ironically also needed them for shelter and security.

There in his cabin on board the Majestic, more than fifty years later Peter came to a realization that had alluded him since childhood. Now he could understand the complex and hidden dynamics of his family. Silence and ignorance would have protected the children not only from unknown sorrow, the sharp inquires of neighbors, but also the possible scrutiny from the dreaded authorities. They couldn't reveal anything they didn't know. That loss of knowing was a price they innocently had to pay.

He realized that fear had become the main motivator in the lives of his family as it was for their entire crippled nation under absolute rule. Now with this greater, deeper understanding he could forgive a mother who didn't inform them, a grandmother who abused them, and a father who left them for one reason or another.

But he would never forgive the Nazis, the National Socialist German Workers Party.

PASSAU

PASSAU, KNOWN AS the city of three rivers, with its pastel-colored buildings and narrow cobblestone streets is a main gateway to Austria and sits at the confluence of land where the Danube, Ilz, and Inn Rivers join. Until the waters mix together in the Danube, they are specifically different in color from one another, depending on their back-country soil conditions. Flooding, however, had always been an issue and all the water levels since 1842 were recorded on a marker at the town hall.

Because of its location at the edge of the frontier, the city had been an important trade route in Roman times, especially significant for the shipping of salt. Now it was still a progressive commercial site with a major university. Its unique setting often found tourists making a stop, especially to see the beautiful rococo cathedral, St. Stephen, and to hear the largest pipe organ in Germany.

When they were docked, Peter saw that a concert was scheduled for that afternoon at the cathedral but Mike and Kari wanted to go on a Danube bike tour that was also advertised. It would take them along the river and back for an abbreviated four to five-hour ride. The oldest such trail in Europe, it was considered by many the best. One could go from Passau all the way to Vienna and Budapest and on to the Black Sea if desired.

It seemed like a good idea to break up the boat trip for the youngsters. Peter couldn't refuse even if it meant for them to miss the concert. Julie also agreed with the request and also quickly agreed she loved organ music so Peter found her at his side as he entered the cathedral. Emma and some of the tour group were also there in the midst of a crowded audience.

The program was an all-Beethoven event with a short early work, the Fugue in D major, written when he was 13 or 14 years old and the only solo piece he ever wrote for organ. It was a smooth, simple, almost soft piece to be followed by his late work, the contrasting, crowning 5th Symphony adapted for organ. It represented the young and the older work of the man, much like the combination of Peter and Mike. The church setting with its beautiful white and gold interior and the thunderous music pleased Peter a great deal.

Afterwards Julie, Peter, Emma and some of the other tour members joined together for a meal at a nearby restaurant. Having *rouladen* and *spatzle* reminded him of the beef rolls and noodles that his grandmother had made on those few special occasions they had. The group lingered long, ordering apple *struddle* and coffee, being happy with full stomachs and ringing musical chords still in their heads.

Julie was seen talking to Emma, rather intensely thought Peter, but what did a man know? It couldn't be about him, of course not. Or could it? Enough of vanity. His rather lined face and stocky build usually didn't get too much attention, even though he had soft hazel eyes and a good head of hair for an older man. Well, so much for that. Then it was time for him to go back to the boat and wait for the cyclists to return.

Peter had just stretched out on the bed for a quick nap

when he heard a soft knock at the door. Surely not Mike yet but it was quickly repeated. Emma stood outside as he opened it up. She was obviously upset.

"Oh, Peter, I'm sorry to disturb you. I have to ask a favor of you."

"Come in, come in. So, what is it?" he said, indicating that she should be seated.

She declined and continued. "Someone has been in my cabin while we were out. They disturbed my things and I'm scared."

"Well, shouldn't you go to the boat's security?"

"Oh, no I can't do that because its... its rather sensitive. The intruder didn't actually take anything but he was looking for the relief money. I'm sure of it."

"So, if he didn't find anything?"

"I can't keep it in my room. He got in some way, with a lock card, I think. He must know about the money. What if he comes back?" She was near tears.

"You'll have to tell security."

"No, that's a problem. That's why I want to ask you. Could you keep some bags in your cabin? No one would be able to figure out where it is."

"Well, Emma, I don't know. I'd like to help you, of course," stammered Peter.

"Oh, that's so good of you." She was now crying and collapsed into a chair. Peter, distressed, came to offer her comfort, reaching for a tissue on the night stand. Then suddenly the grief-stricken face of his sister Anna came to him. For years he had pushed aside the guilt and he tried unsuccessfully to do so again. Perhaps helping Emma was a way of atonement now for that sad imbedded memory.

A soldier had come to their apartment to investigate

rumors of missing coal. Only he and his sister were home at the time as all the others were at the market picking up their rationed goods. The man might suspect him of stealing, of course, so he hid quickly in the standing wardrobe. He was an eleven-year-old boy frozen with fear.

He stayed there even as he heard strange noises and furniture being moved. His sister's cry made him peak out for a moment but the soldier's laugh made him retreat quickly inside again. He remained there long after he heard the door slamming. When the others returned, he came out to a scene of frenzy with all of them huddled around Anna. She wasn't sobbing but her dress looked messy, her hair tangled and her eyes wild. The man had hurt or frightened her, no doubt, and her brother should have done something about it but he didn't or couldn't.

The shattering memory shook him back to reality when her heard Emma say, "Thanks so much! I knew you'd understand."

"But, but…Of course I think I understand, Emma," he stammered, her voice and likeness to Anna blurring his thoughts. "But it's rather unusual, isn't it?"

"Yes, yes but it's a favor, Peter. Please, please."

"Well. I suppose I could do it. I could put it in my safe. I haven't used it. Couldn't you use your safe?"

"No, it's rather large," she said, quickly getting up from the chair and going to the door. "I'll be right back."

Peter stood stunned and hadn't recovered when she, still with tear stains on her face, abruptly returned, carrying two canvass souvenir bags which both seemed filled.

"Oh, my God. Is that all money?"

"No, no, not exactly. They're packed, so no one can see what's in them. That's why he didn't find it, I believe," she explained,

"Well, let me see what you have here."

Peter sorted out the contents, getting a surprise when he withdrew women's sanitary napkins. He stopped and looked at her.

"That's probably why he didn't look any further," she said.

"Presuming the intruder was a man?"

"Oh, I should think so." She almost smiled, wiping her face dry.

In the midst of the package, Peter saw the money rolls. Many money rolls, many more that had been in the tote bag, for sure. "Is the other bag like this one?"

"Yes. You could store them under the sink, a logical place for them. That's where I had them." She hugged him close and he smiled. "Thank you so much. You're a dear. You know we can't lose the relief money. They're counting on us."

"I don't know about this," he said weakly.

"It will be all right, I'm sure. I trust you, you're so honest. When we get to Budapest, I'll take them back. No problem." She seemed entirely at ease now but Peter was floundering as he picked up the bags and went to the bathroom.

"Thanks again. See you later. Bye," she said as she flew out the door.

Peter stood dazed. All that money. Surely thousands of Euros. He could take it and spend it but she trusted him to keep it safe. What did that all mean? There was now an even more considerable amount in the bags under the faucet then they had previously seen. Could he be held accountable? Had he just been duped? And what should he tell Mike? When the boy, looking rather sweaty, came in Peter made the decision. He'd discuss the matter later when he could decide what to say.

"So, how was it along the river?" he asked.

"She is older than me," said Mike, disgusted.

"What the river?"

"No, Kari. She told me she's almost thirteen." It was a strong statement.

"Oh, terrific, that makes her about twelve then, I would guess. Mike, I was asking about your adventure, your bike trip."

"Oh, it was great. Only rained a bit at the beginning."

Peter left out a sigh. Somehow this wasn't the response he had expected. "Can you tell me what you saw or did?"

"We rode on the path which is just next to the river and sometimes the road. It was very easy going but there were lots of people out actually. Skate boarders, some runners, even families pushing baby buggies. It must be used a lot."

"So, was it fun?

"Yah, real fun. We had a blast, that is until she told me about her age. I wish we could have gone further because the scenery was great, Gramps. Houses and gardens, hills nearby. The river was busy too with barges and boats, you know."

Somehow this still wasn't what Peter expected. Where was his insightful young grandson? Too busy fussing over Kari. "I guess I'll have to ask the almost thirteen-year-old for more precise descriptions."

"She'd tell you all right. She's good at describing things but I'm tired and hungry. Do you think the snack bar is still open on the ship?"

"I would think so. Why don't you go get something? I'm not hungry. We had a great meal after the concert. Too bad you missed it."

"What? The concert or the meal?"

"Both, but go on. I'll interrogate you again later about your fabulous experience."

Mike caught his grandfather's displeasure. "It was great, really, Gramps. Thanks so much. I mean it. We even got to Austria. It isn't far from here."

And they did get to Austria shortly after leaving Passau, complete with houses and gardens, even barges and boats coming and going. In fact, the emerging Wachau Valley was spectacular for its natural beauty with vineyards terraced up the hillsides above small colorful villages and medieval castles, Austria's counter balance to the Rhine Valley. It also has been designated as a World Heritage Site.

At Durnstein, with its blue church, they saw a castle ruin high above, the site where Richard the Lion Hearted had been imprisoned in 1193. He had gone from England to fight in the crusades and on his way home, Duke Leopold of Austria had him imprisoned there. He only gained his freedom after a huge ransom was paid for his return.

They passed by other historic towns and landmarks along the way with thousand-year-old vineyards clinging to the hillsides. Krems with its Renaissance and Medieval buildings was once an important trading center. There the Benedictine Abbey was still in operation after 900 years. At St. Michel, the fortified church was the site of the first Christian house of worship from the 900's and where the Turks and then the Protestants were driven out to establish this Catholic area. At Spitz, the Hinterhaus castle ruins stood high up on a ridge over the town.

"Just history everywhere," said Peter as they stretched out on the deck to view the passing scene. He was enjoying a glass of apricot wine, the local specialty, and the warm sunlight on his face. "Too bad we aren't going to stop at Melk. I'd like to see the monastery and the library." He had often read about the collection of its 100,000 books, many of them important manuscripts from the Middle Ages saved by the monks.

Later, as they passed Melk, the ship slowed and cruised near the shore, allowing the passengers to see the stunning yellow façade of the large abbey with its twin towers and octagonal dome, all reflected in the waters of the river. Peter took some photos. Emma on the intercom elaborated more about the history of the structure which had been built in 1297 and the victim of fire several times with the present building built in 1702. Other architectural significant features included a pink marble stairway and frescoes.

Mike said, "I'm getting a little confused with all these churches and stuff. Every place seems to have one or two of them, some very much alike."

"Remember these towns have been here for hundreds of years and have been influenced by similar factors like religion or the government. Our towns are pretty much alike too, only newer and not so picturesque probably."

"You're right. We all have drive-ins like McDonalds and the strip malls with their hair salons and fitness gyms. And the grocery chains look the same everywhere."

"Don't forget the big furniture stores and the car dealerships spreading for miles."

The summation seemed to end that profound discussion with Mike returning to be the amazing little observer without the distraction from Kari. Being uncomfortable in the sun, the boy decided he was ready for a shower. He disappeared and Peter was left to contemplate. He closed his eyes and time passed, the nice thing about a cruise. Being reminded of America, his thoughts turned to Margie and the girls. What would they be doing now? Was everything ok at home? He thought about Hawkins College and realized how removed he now felt from it, casually cruising down the Danube.

The time of being a classroom teacher had been fulfilling for him. He'd enjoyed the interaction with the students, always working with conversational language for them to get comfortable in the foreign tongue. He wanted to represent the German world as progressive and democratic, shying away from the fascist years that he had known.

As department chair, he actively sponsored study abroad to many countries in connection with a local non-profit that helped to supply scholarships. He often thought about his early struggling years being limited in educational opportunities and how hard it was to fit into another language. Seeing the increasing importance of global knowledge through language skills, he fought for increasing classes, even while required modern language studies were being eliminated by administrators.

He and his staff worked hard to make the courses appealing in order to retain their student enrollment. His knowledge of European higher education's focus on language inspired him. It was always an impressive moment when on a foreign trip he encountered so many accomplished English speakers. Of course, the trades people in Europe usually didn't have that advantage, being the product of separated systems in their early education. In America, the chance for language learning wasn't separated but also wasn't encouraged and often not seen as needed.

Like most American schools, Spanish became the dominate language study for obvious reasons but in recent years he was proud of increasing the reach of exposure in his department with a Chinese woman who taught Mandarin. He also developed during his tenure at Hawkins a lively cultural scene with the department holding ethnic fairs.

foreign movies, global music, and food booths featuring

delicious regional fare. It had been fun earning his living that way and the years had flown by fast.

However, Mike was suddenly beside him, his head and wide eyes staring in his face. "Gramps, what do we have in the bathroom? I saw these bags. What are they?"

The moment had come. Peter straightened up and cleared his throat. "I'm storing some things for Emma. Doing her a favor."

"But what are those things?" The boy was in a serious quandary, taking out some pads.

"Well, they're feminine items. I hope you know about ladies and their... essentials."

"Essentials?"

"Actually, the truth is that they're just the covering, the protection." Peter felt the conversation was coming out wrong.

"Protection?"

"Yes, yes for the money that Emma has. You know we were going to keep it quiet. Well, she asked me to hide the bags in our room. She had some intrusion into her room and she was scared about the money."

It took a moment to sink in for Mike. Then out of the mouth of babes, he said the obvious. "That seems pretty strange."

"Yes, I agree but I got kind of stuck when she asked me."

"I knew it. I can't leave you alone, Gramps. The ladies are after you and I promised Gramsy that I'd take good care of you. Remember?" He was proudly laughing.

"Yes, my boy. I remember and don't you worry. Its' nothing like that." Peter laughed too but the imagine of Emma's pretty face, awash in tears came to him. Earlier she had shared her family's story about their desire to help the refugees. She had seemed so sincere that she was hard to refuse.

"Gramps, Kari and I are going on a ship tour. They said it

was a special deal just for kids. We get to see the captain on the bridge and the prep work in the kitchen."

"Sounds great. Glad you are still kids. I've got to finish cleaning up the stuff in the crates. I think I'll need another bag to carry everything. I can't seem to part with most of it."

"They sell some nice souvenir bags in the gift shop. You know, just the kind that Emma had."

"A good idea. I'll get one."

Kari appeared at the door and the two youngsters took off for their tour while Peter went to buy a bag. Coming back with a sturdy one that had Majestic logos on it, he settled down and revisited the contents. He put the original photos in the cookie tin and placed it at the bottom of the bag. The books that he'd saved and the loose reprints filled up the rest. He would hand carry it with him on the way home. Somehow the thought of bringing those photos and items of the past comforted him.

He could accept the fact that he might not ever know his father's complete story but he was willing to think well of him now. Many had lost loved ones during those times, never to be seen again, but he had gained some insight about his father. Because of the photos, he would choose to regard him as a man of tragedy, even possibly a hero against the Nazi regime. He was no longer a vague dark image and it pleased him.

Thinking about it again, in other times and circumstances, he might have been in line at the family business here in Germany. He would have seen success as the country rebuilt into a modern nation. He might have been content with that as were his cousins and friend Klaus. But he didn't regret his turn in history, despite his troubling early years. Something in him had changed in America.

He looked again at the small worn Bible and thought of his mother's trials, not only the struggles during and after the war but also when she had breast cancer. In those days, having only limited medicine and fewer treatment options, it left her a vulnerable victim. Erma's first surgery and treatment brought her remission but the disease returned deadly again later. Then it was worse because the morphine available no longer eased the pain. Her quiet personality was changed to loud moans in the night that often disturbed his sleep.

When he left for America, he knew she was terminal but it was her definite desire that he should go and go without guilt. She said knowing he was safe in America was the only wish left in her life. Her insistence showed in her smile, perhaps the last time she managed it, and that image stayed with him for years. It was a blessing.

He opened the book up to Psalms. The worn page of the 23rd Psalm must have given her comfort. *"Yea, though I walk through the valley of the shadows of death, I will fear no evil: for thou art with me, thy rod and thy staff they comfort me. Thou preparest a table before me in the presence of mine enemies: thou anointest my head with oil: my cup runneth over. Surely goodness and mercy shall follow me all the days of my life: and I will dwell in the house of the LORD forever."*

As she had hoped, he did find a safe haven in America and did find another blessing in his life – Margie, his wife, who made him happy to be alive.

VIENNA

WIEN, THE FORMER capital of the Austro-Hungarian Empire, is often called the city of music. Beethoven, Mozart, Strauss and so many others filled the years with melodies, famous around the world. The city of almost two million lays close to the Czech, Slovakian, and Hungarian border and had retained its sophisticated reputation as a center of the arts and science through the years. Many films, like "The Third Man" and the James Bond series were made in and around its lovely classical buildings.

Its history goes back to Roman and Medieval times. The damage from World War II was gone but memories of the 200,000 Jews living there before the war still lingered. Many had fled or were eliminated and after that only 5,000 remained. With the Soviet occupation, it then became noted as a center for intrigue and spies between the East and West.

Modern tourism was important and like many visitors, Peter and Mike started the day with a ride along the three-mile long *Ringstrasse* on the old boundary of the city wall which was torn down in 1857. They passed by important buildings: Parliament, Imperial Palace and the Opera House. The next stop was at the *Stephansdom* with its designed roof of unusual glazed tile. Although destroyed in the war, its restoration was amazing and one of the most recognized features of Vienna.

They enjoyed the morning tour but Peter regretfully planned a break for the afternoon one which showcased the magnificent palaces of the Belvidere, a summer residence with magnificent gardens, and the seventieth century *Schoenbrunn* with its 1441 rooms that were located outside the inner city. He, thinking Mike had seen enough of churches and palaces, instead scheduled a visit to the Spanish Riding School, home of the famous white Lipizzan horses where a dressage performance was scheduled. They arrived in time to see the men in black uniforms atop their gallant white steeds going through the jumps and turns, all in perfect coordination. It was thrilling for Mike because he had always admired horses, even though he'd never had any experience with them.

"I'd love to get a horse someday but my mother said if we had an apartment of our own, we could get a dog."

"I'll help you. A boy needs a dog," his grandfather said.

Close to Peter's heart was their next event. When he arrived in Vienna all those years ago, all the group wanted to do was to have a ride on the *Reisenrad*, that glorious Ferris Wheel, built in 1877, 212 feet tall and one of the highest in the world with 30 enclosed gondolas. It was every kid's dream but they were to be disappointed. No time for such things in war time and they were told that it wasn't running anyway, because of damage.

Now he could ride with his grandson, because it was fully restored and still functioning, one of the few of that vintage in the world. And so up and around they went. The man and boy were equally thrilled with the experience as the city landscape spread beneath them. They giggled almost like girls with Mike saying, "I'll have to tell Aunt Tracy about this. She digs amusement parks."

The day was getting on and Peter wanted to see one more thing before they went back to the Majestic. He wanted to show Mike a real crazy place known as the Hundertwasser house. It was the creation by the architect of 52 ridiculously assembled apartments built in 1983 with sloping roofs and wavy sides, crazy bright colors of blue and gold, and fantastic mixture of decorations, inside and out. It also had a grass roof and trees that grew inside of rooms, poking their branches outside. All done on purpose for the design.

"Too bad I don't have my sketch pad with me. Now this is a place that Kari would love," said Mike. And magically she appeared skipping down the sidewalk. Panting a bit behind her was Julie, who with her patterned smock, blazing scarf and jewelry seemed a real natural as part of the lopsided scene. It was a fun reunion and they laughed all the way back to the ship.

Upon returning Peter needed to use the bathroom facilities so he hurried ahead of the rest. Upon opening the door, he sensed something unusual but hurrying, he went directly to the bathroom and switched on the light, leaving the door ajar. Several sanitary napkins were on the floor and he knew immediately what it was. Someone had found the money!

He whirled about and saw a figure attempting to flee the bedroom. With a big effort, he jumped around, slamming against the man who dropped a duffel bag he was carrying.

It was Roger Twilling.

"What's going on here?" Peter shouted, knowing full well the answer, as he felt a stunning blow to his shoulder. The men grappled against one another and Peter slipped down, pulling at Roger's jacket. Then he saw the gun being pulled out of the pocket and immediately he released his hold and stumbled backwards.

"You weren't supposed to be here," said Roger gruffly, leveling the weapon at Peter. "But now I have to do something with you."

"For God's sake, Roger, what in the world are you...," he tried to continue just as Mike came in from the hall.

"Gramps!"

Roger turned momentarily and Peter plunged forward like lightning and tried to grab the gun. However, Roger swaying, held fast and the gun fired, sending the bullet to the ceiling. They struggled but Mike, now seeing the situation, instinctively kicked Roger's leg hard.

"God damn kid," howled Roger, loosening his grip slightly on the weapon because of the distraction. Peter successfully pulled it away.

"I've got it now," said Peter. "Up against the wall, Roger."

Instead, Roger lunged forward, knocking them both to the floor and sending the gun flying away. It landed beside the door just as Julie was coming in. With a startled cry, she saw the men on the floor with Mike also jumping on top of Roger in the melee. Also seeing the gun, she grabbed it with one scoop and aimed it at the wrestling combatants

"Stop! Gentlemen, stop! Take it easy. I've got a gun pointed at you and I know how to use it," she yelled. The movement stopped. "What's going on?" she demanded.

Peter, breathing hard, said, "He was robbing me."

"Well, then Roger, you stay on the floor. Roll over. Face down," she ordered briskly as Peter and Mike controlled the squirming Roger, forcing his hands behind his back.

Just then Karen came into the room and cried out, "What's happening?"

"Karen, take off my scarf and give it to Michael," Julie ordered her niece with urgency but without lessoning her stance. The Carrot did as she was told in almost robot-like motion. Mike, getting the idea, immediately tied Roger's hands with the silk scarf and pulled it hard while Peter continued to hold the squirming man down.

"Karen, call the office for security. Quick!" ordered Julie again.

The Carrot was on the room phone in a second and pushed the button. "Hello, hello. We need help. Come to room 165. We've had a fight here."

"Tell them it was a robbery," said Peter, pushing his knee harder against Roger in case the scarf didn't hold.

"I mean a robbery. Come quick," she responded.

Mike got up, giving Kari a special smile, as he kicked the duffel bag away. Otherwise, the tableau remained silent, unmoving until the ship's security guard, with hand cuffs jingling, arrived.

"So, what do we have here?" he asked, looking at the arrangement on the floor and also giving a sharp look at Julie who now dropped the gun to her side.

"Here, you probably want the gun. It's only fired one shot, I believe," she said. "Not by me."

The guard examined it and slid it under his belt. After fastening the cuffs on Roger, he removed the scarf and then forced him to stand up. "I've seen lots of restraints but never one quite like this."

"Sorry, it's the best we could do at the moment," said Julie calmly, kneeling down to pick up her scarf.

There was noise in the hallway as neighbors suddenly appeared and crowded around to see what the turmoil was about. The guard shooed them away as Roger shouted, as in explanation, "It was such a temptation. A temptation, you've got to understand." Without hesitation, the guard with Roger in tow swiftly made their way down the hall.

"Wow, Julie, you really were something," said the astonished Peter.

"Oh, it's nothing," she said assuredly. "Not my first rodeo,
as they say." Peter agreed silently to himself that this Julie must
been around the block a few times. Such quick thinking must
have been learned somewhere.

"Mike, you weren't so bad, yourself," said the admiring
Kari, squeezing his arm.

"Yes, now that's what I really call teamwork," said Peter.
"But excuse me, I really do need to use the bathroom." He
quickly slipped into the room, closing the door. The remaining participants all relaxed, slumping down on the chairs and
the bed. Peter re-emerged shortly, after also picking up the
discarded debris on the bathroom floor. Afterward, the door
from the hall opened and in came the ship's Captain and
Emma who had heard the emergency call.

"How are you all doing?" he questioned them, seeing
their strained faces. "The guard will be placing the man in
our secure lock up on board and I'll call for the authorities
in Vienna who assist us with these situations. We're so sorry
about this incident but you don't have to worry. They'll be
here to investigate and process the case but I need your name
and particulars. This is your room, correct?"

Peter immediately responded, giving everyone's name.
"We caught Roger in my room here. He was in the process of
robbing me." Peter looked around the room, now first noticing drawers opened and bed clothes in disarray, and then he
saw Emma's frantic worried look. "You can see the place is
disheveled, the end result of that for yourself. We had a tussle
and he took a shot at me. The bullet is in the ceiling there. But
I definitely had help taking him down."

"Are you injured?"

"Oh, no, no. Just a little scratch here I notice."

"What were the items stolen and any other damage that you can see?"

"He got the money that I had lying around, I believe, and important documents in that travel tote," added Peter, pointing to his family photos and papers spilled on the floor. He didn't mention the duffel bag and gave Emma a reassuring smile. "But we intercepted him so I don't think he got away with anything significant."

"That's good but we need to have a record of the incident. Armed intrusion. Write down a record when you summarize everything. We'll repair the ceiling," he said looking around and glancing in the bathroom and closet. "I see the safe hasn't been opened."

"No, I didn't use it. It wasn't big enough for all our valuables, anyway." said Peter quickly. "We have antiques and art works."

Mike opened his mouth questioning but a stern look from Peter hushed him.

"Well, you can store your valuables in a large secure locker we have in the hold. Just bring them down to the information desk and we'll take care of you. Again, I'm so very sorry about this experience aboard the Majesty". The man seemed satisfied and said to Emma, "You help them settle in for tonight but please keep this event a low profile from the other guests."

"Certainly, sir.," she said as he left

Mike broke in. "Gramps, since when do we have antiques and art?"

"Just a slight exaggeration. Your mother's tapestry, the prints and your sketches," Peter said laughing. Looking at Emma and then the duffel bag, he said, "We need better security."

"Oh, God," Emma said, "I didn't know they had any secure lockers. I knew I couldn't use their vault because I'm really not part of the ship's crew."

"Well, it seems they will serve us now." Peter changed course. "Julie, I can't thank you enough but you and Karen deserve a rest, I think, after this exciting incident. We'll join you later at dinner after we clean up this place. Ok?"

With raised eyebrows about this apparent dismissal, Julie pulled Kari away as they left. Emma stayed behind, wanting to say something but not able to speak for a bit. "I'm sure the police will be here soon. They may check out the room and question the witnesses."

"Mike, pack up our fancy antiques, will you? Let's get the rest of the stuff down to the lockers," he said grabbing the duffel bag. He opened it up, allowing Emma to see the money inside and being satisfied, they smiled. He carefully replaced the papers and photos in the tote. Obviously, Roger had rummaged through it but hadn't found anything valuable there. But he had indeed found Emma's bags under the sink and filled his duffel bag.

"I hope that Julie and Kari didn't see the duffel. She is such a nosey body, always spying on people. By the way, how did Roger get in the room?" she asked.

The answer appeared as they looked about. The sliding door to the balcony was slightly open.

"I guess we forgot to lock it, "said Mike.

"You're right. Not your fault." Peter paused. "And investing reporters have ways to find loop holes and follow leads, even to climb over balconies and hop in windows."

"I would never have thought Roger capable of this," said Emma quietly. "But he had a gun and was ready to use it.

That's some forethought."

"He did use the good cover of a respectable journalist."

They took the duffel bag and filled a suitcase with souvenirs and clothing to the office but he left the tote bag with the photos in the room. It wasn't interesting to anyone but himself. They got the key and Peter gave it to Emma as she left. She seemed to pause with indecision.

"It's your money, as I said before," Peter said. "Just leave the locker open later when you take the duffel bag so we can get our luggage. After all this, I do hope the money does some good for the refugees."

"Oh, yes" she said. Then with a different tone, she added, "You have returned it to me once before. Amazing. I'm grateful. Thanks."

"God, Gramps, this is all too much," Mike said after she left. "But I'm dying for food."

They were off to the dining room, the farewell dinner completely forgotten because of the recent event but they were back within minutes to change clothes. They both fussed about what to wear as dressy attire was expected and their selection didn't extend to that level. Mike resorted to his new t shirt from Heidelberg and Pater chose a simple white shirt. "I hope they let us in but there is going to be some hard looks, that's for sure," Peter said.

"Can you imagine what Julie will think?" Mike replied.

They managed the challenge and sat in a corner table to avoid being obvious and then Julie and Kari, done up to the t's in shimmering splendor, came in. Julie made a sudden sharp turn to the middle of the room when she saw them. Certainly not up to her standards. Kari raised her hands in resignation, smiling broadly with shinning silver braces complimenting her outfit. They also spotted Emma at the head table.

Never the less, they enjoyed the special helping of Weiner schnitzel, red cabbage, fried potatoes and a generous chocolate portion of *sache torte*. There was singing from a German-Austrian trio, an ensemble of shoe tapping dancers and a polka band at the end. It was so enjoyable they almost forgot about the break-in.

Later they were visited by the shore police who had just come from interviewing the captain. They repeated the outline of the incident and Peter signed a certified document of their testimony. As they were international travelers, they would not have to appear personally in court on Roger's charges of armed robbery and personal attack. The Majesty's legal team would press the charge.

The men also shared some quick information they had found about Roger, verifying that indeed he was an American journalist living in Europe for many years. They had also tracked down his past publishing credits, noting his bylines of many stories during the fall of the wall and other unique insights into Eastern Germany, the DDR. afterward. However, they had found no evidence of articles for the past two years.

"He must have fallen on hard times," they surmised upon leaving.

"Yes, that could be it," agreed Peter.

Mike pulled out his sketch book and started to draw the outline of the room and balcony door. Peter stretched out on the bed, his mind racing. He said, "I'm just going to settle in for the night. It's been quite a day and I need to think it all through."

So, Roger wasn't a fake, but why did he turn to robbery? He'd openly admitted investigating the money trail intended for the refugee assistance. But was he in that great a need of money himself? He'd apparently not published for some time.

Why not? There must have been a problem. Then temptation came in front of him. He said so himself.

He arose from the bed and went to check the doors before getting ready for bed. This brought on another question. How did he know the money was here? Had he also been the one to ransack Emma's room? Probably. The feminine pads were the clue. He hadn't disturbed them earlier but seeing them here, so out of place in a man's room, was the answer to finding the money.

"Why and how did he come to this room in the first place?" he questioned himself again out loud.

"Oh, that's easy," said Mike. "He saw us with Emma a lot, I bet. Lots of people did, like Julie and Kari. He figured we must be part of the operation. When he couldn't find the money in her room, he put two and two together."

"Yes, how stupid of me to get involved in this sort of thing. I can't believe I did that."

"You were just trying to help her," said Mike, sounding very comforting and grown up. "It's like what you said, that thing you do to make up for something else you did but shouldn't have."

"Atonement. "

"Yah, that's it."

Peter was surprised at his grandson's simple insight. His sister's-stricken face came to him. And then Emma's tearful plea. He actually did feel that connection.

"But there's still something fishy about it all," he acknowledged.

"Well, we're out of it now, right?"

"Yes, hopefully. And hopefully we can get some sleep tonight," Peter said as he rolled over into the covers. But hope didn't bring him peaceful sleep. The day's anxiety twirled in his mind, mixed with long ago shadows of danger. Again, he heard the sirens, the bombers whining overhead and then his sister's scream. He tossed and turned. The word, rape, came to him. As a young boy, he had only learned much later what rape actually meant and that it was a crime.

Then Mike's face appeared. He awoke. Mike didn't hide in the closet. No, the kid had immediately defended his grandfather, helped save him by kicking Roger's leg. Unlike that little boy of long ago, he wouldn't have to atone for his inaction. That brought Peter pride about Mike and comfort for his own guilt which was now softened, finally allowing a deep sleep to overcome him.

BUDAPEST

IT WAS A clear sunny day as the boat arrived at Budapest, the capital of Hungary and the former co-capital of the Austrian-Hungarian Empire. Emma's voice came on strong. "As we near Budapest, called the Queen of the Danube or Paris of the East, you can see that the city of near two million inhabitants is divided into two sections by the Danube River. Pest of the left, Buda on the right, combined together in 1872."

"You might say we saved the best river view for the last day of your journey Before you on the right you see at the edge of the river the seat of the government, the famous Parliament Building, started in 1885 and opened in 1902. Isn't it a marvelous sight? It's especially impressive when lit at night?"

Emma continued, "Imre Steindl was the architect of this Gothic and Renaissance masterpiece, which contains only 365 towers and 691 rooms." She laughed. "Some of its most glorious features are the main staircase, the dome and the Hungarian Holy Crown which has crowned 50 kings. Of course, Hungary still conducts business here after the 1956 revolution against the communist state."

"Across the river is the Fisherman's Bastion, with its seven towers celebrating the seven ancient tribes. Ahead you will see the long suspension Chain Bridge. It was the first permanent bridge across the Danube, built in 1849. And now we're almost ready to depart."

The Majestic slowed and stopped. The passengers started to gather on the deck. Emma's voice came on again, sounding like a canned speech. "On behalf of Wonder World Tours and the Majesty with its wonderful staff, let me personally thank you for joining us on this adventure. We enjoyed having you on board and wish you all a safe journey home. As you depart, be sure you have all your personal items with you. If you enrolled in one of the extensions, you'll have two more days of sightseeing by local guides in Budapest. The busses will arrive shortly to take you to your designated hotels. Your luggage which was collected this morning will be delivered by van to those locations."

There was enthusiastic applause from the crowd. Mike added a whistle. Peter smiled because the boy showed so much exuberance. He even seemed taller. He probably was, with all the food he had put down, but his frame didn't show any sidewards expansion. Definitely, the trip had been good for him. He saw Mike wave to Carrot in the crowd and they met, sitting down at a nearby table.

Vans were already parked on the dock. While waiting for the busses to arrive, Peter continued to stand at the rail, watching the activity below as the gang plank was lowered. Immediately crew members hauled out carts filled with luggage and loaded them into the vans. A large freight truck was parked nearby to pick up the debris and garbage from the ship.

Peter then noticed a small police van behind the truck. He frowned, questioning, as he saw two uniformed men get out and briskly come up the gang plank. Could it be another robbery? Or something worse? Goodness, not more drama?

The vans were now leaving and the tourist busses were lining up. The crowd started moving toward the exit. Peter waved to Mike to come along. He was busy showing Carrot his sketches and then he tore one out of his pad and gave it to her. Peter couldn't tell what it was but thought he saw the flash of braises when she smiled. It made him smile too.

Suddenly Aunt Julie appeared, her scarves flying. "We're off then," she declared breathlessly. "Going directly to the airport. We've sent our luggage ahead. I'm through with all this and Karen has to get back. But Peter, I understand you're staying on for a couple more days."

"Yes, that's right. Give Mike here a glimpse of Budapest before we go home."

Catching Peter by the sleeve, Julie gave him a quick hearty hug and turning to Mike, she managed a robust kiss on his cheek. Mike gasped uneasily and Peter shook his head in amusement but it was an awkward moment for the youngsters. With eyes sadly downcast, they squeezed hands as they parted. Julie pulled her niece away and they scurried to a waiting taxi.

Peter suddenly caught sight of Emma ahead of him in the crowd. She wasn't carrying her umbrella or her tote bag. The two officers were walking close by her side, one of them holding a large clip board and a duffel bag, looking heavily laden. He hurried to reach her but they got lost in the crowd and then he saw them walking to the police vehicle. He ran toward them and she saw him, turning slightly as she was assisted into the back of the van. She raised her hand in a weak wave. She wasn't smiling.

He stopped, unsure. The door was closed, locked as he heard a loud click. The officers immediately got in the vehicle and it rolled forward and out of the lot. What did he just see?

Turning, he saw Mike coming after him, a strange look on his face.

"What was that?"

"I'm not sure. They just took Emma away in that van. Locked her in."

They both stood still for a long moment in deliberation and then realized that most of the passengers had already boarded the busses.

"We've got to go."

And they did, sitting together in stunned silence on the way to their hotel. Once in the room, Mike said, "She must have done something really wrong."

"Obviously."

"Do you think it had to do with the money?"

"It's almost always about money." Peter shrugged his shoulders, unwilling to believe it. Mike probably hadn't seen the duffel bag they carried out but Peter knew what it contained. It must have something to do with a crime. Certainly not with relief efforts. What and why? His mind swirled with possibilities. There must have been some tip off about the money. Who? Possibly Roger in custody? Who else? Someone on the boat? He took a very long pause, thinking about his aiding and abetting a criminal act, even if he were innocently involved?

Then shaking himself free of that complication, he said, "Let's leave it there for now, Mike. We can't figure it out at the moment. Besides we have to get ready for the city tour. We're to meet in the lobby in half an hour."

Mike asked, "Why can't we go to the place where you were camped out during the war?"

"Traveling to that area is now restricted because of the Bosnian conflict. And anyway, the estate is no longer there.

Don't know what it looks like now. All destroyed and then divided up after the communistic take-over." Peter thought again quietly about his visit to the former owner, Herr Redmann, in Detroit. The man had expressed no interest in returning again to his homeland, saying the buildings and memories were all gone, swept away just like a tornado hit it.

Peter continued, "When I came here before, I really didn't get to see much of Budapest because it was just a place to transfer to a rail line which took us to lower Hungary. I do remember seeing the Parliament building from the boat and thought its spires were beautiful. It's a lot like London's Parliament. We'll get to see more today, I'm sure."

A unique tour did indeed await them but they were only passive observers, still much too stunned from the incident during departure to appreciate the sights. They had signed up for a ride around the city with a special guide in a Trabi, the famous small car used in the Eastern Bloc countries under Soviet rule. In modern times it was only an historical object of tourist interest.

St. Stephen Basilica, the largest church in Budapest, was impressive, causing Mike to wonder why so many churches were named after St. Stephen. "Who was that Stephen, anyway? They had a church in Vienna and in Passau."

"He was the first martyr of Christianity. Being against the temple cult, he was stoned to death for his faith. Perhaps people in this region have a bond with him as they have often been victims of opposing beliefs over the ages."

They crossed the river to the Castle District and Mike got out his sketch book to quickly note the passing scenes. Peter also clicked his camera as they drove past Buda Castle, originally the home of Hungarian kings, and now a rebuilt museum after being gutted from World War II damage. Although they didn't get a chance to visit inside on the drive-by, they were given a leg stretch outside, providing them a splendid view of the entire city.

They saw St. Matthias Church, a grand Gothic structure with painted domes, that was used for the coronation of kings. Fisherman's Bastion, the favorite landmark above the Danube with its seven towers representing seven tribes, was the last site before being driven to their hotel.

"Let's go to the baths, Mike, to relax," suggested Peter when they returned.

"What's with that? Baths?"

"Yes, Budapest is also known for its many springs and steam baths."

"How about something to eat? I'm hungry."

"Oh, of course, I should have known."

Off they went to discover another interesting feature of the city. Ruin bars, with damaged walls brimming with bright colored retro décor, actual wrecked cars filled with all sorts of merchandise, and loud music, provided the menu of Hungarian goulash and mashed potatoes. Having their fill, they walked off their dinner to the city's huge *Szecenyi* thermal baths which were surrounded by classical buildings and lovely landscape features. The information on the entrance sign was written in Hungarian, of course, and they could not read it.

"Oh, good, they have a translation in German," said Peter. "The Magyar language or Hungarian is difficult."

"I thought you were a language teacher, Gramps. You could read everything else along the trip."

"Yes, but this one if different. It's a separate system entirely from other European languages. They had few foreign language influences, partially because of their early isolation.

It used some loan words from the Turks, Slavs, even some German but it remains an isolated pattern."

"So, what does it say in German?"

"Well, the city has 118 natural springs, pumping out 13 million mineral rich gallons of water every day. There are 15 public outdoor baths with more private ones in various hotels. Used as early as Roman times, future plans include enhancing more special features like special massage areas, etc."

"So how do we get to swim?"

"We can rent our suits, flip flops and towels but we're really in luck tonight. It says they have special spa parties called "*sparties*" every Saturday night." After getting their outfits, they took a quick splash into the pool, then just soaked up the setting at the edge as they watched the "*sparties*" all around them. It was a pretty wild scene with loud Balkan music, people dancing beside the pool and lots of laughing at the side beer bars in addition to any number of wet and wonderful antics in the water.

"What a great way to end our day," said Mike on the way back. Indeed, it certainly helped elevate the mood of the two. Letters were waiting for them at the hotel. The first one was from Margie but had been forwarded from Vienna. He opened her thick letter with anticipation.

Dearest Peter,

I hope this reaches you at the hotel on the itinerary. Hopefully you found Klaus in good health and spirits. I trust that Mike and you are getting along OK. Here we are doing fairly well, missing you so (especially at night!) and very anxious to see you both again. Will I even recognize you again?

My main concerns, as you know, are with Mother.

She hasn't had a bad scene like the one before you left, but I see her declining rapidly. Physically somewhat, but still manageable for me. But mentally she doesn't want to talk much, even when prodded and I urge the girls to spend time with her, talking about when they were little. She seems to respond to that the best. But they're only here after work so she is tired by then. She doesn't even want to answer my inquires or reflections about my youth at all, making me sad.

I know that her depression can be typical for her age and situation. The social worker suggested using the Senior Day Care Center for daily stimulation with others of her age. So, I took her there last week but it was a terrible experience. About this, she talked readily, accusing me of putting her away with old ugly people. I thought it might improve with more time there, like just one or two days a week, but she wouldn't come out of her room after that, fearing, I'm sure, that I was taking her back to that place. We'll go along with this situation for now but she'll definitely need a nursing facility soon. It is easier to let her be (but I fear wrong), rather than forcing anything on her. Truthfully the quiet hours when she is resting and everyone else is gone gives me time for my garden and reading. I'm grateful for that break but so look forward to your council.

Much has happened with the girls since you left. Tracy got a job at the rec center, doing check-in, taking ID photos, etc. She likes it but spends all her free time socializing with her friends, going to every film and concert there is, spending her money.

Nothing saved for her next semester. That isn't what we had in mind for her summer job. Very spoiled, I'd say but I hate to scold her as this is probably her last summer at home.

Then there is Susan. Her training session went well and she has now settled in to working at the office. Not much of social life for her since most of her old friends have moved on or away. She frets about Mike and misses him. This led up to apartment hunting after work which occupies her almost every day. Fortunately, she likes one nearby.

However, the big news is that Mike's father surfaced last week, having some business in Chicago apparently. He came here unannounced, wanting to see Mike but apparently not Susan as she was at work. As you know, he dropped out of sight when she got custody of Mike and they hadn't been in touch. Obviously, he didn't know that his son was off to Europe with you.

He was visibly disappointed, I would say. Nothing to be done about Mike as he was gone. However, I gave him assurances that when you return, he can come again. But he has to call ahead as visitation is defined by court order, according to Susan. I'm not sure how she will handle it but I think it is a positive move. I think a boy should be able to see his father. I'm sure you agree and we can sort things out when you return.

Another point. I met your old friend, Otto Schwartz, the other day and he was hoping you would be interested in part time volunteering with him at the Immigration Center down town. Sounds like something you would like in retirement.

I'm imagining your fabulous journey and can't wait for your return to hear all about it.

With all my love,

Margie.

He read the letter again. The situation wasn't exactly critical but it disturbed him. The warm feeling after their swim disappeared. Being a hemisphere away didn't help him from feeling lonely. He hung his head to his knees, wanting to be home and holding Margie in his arms, sharing the news together.

"Hey, Gramps, what's the matter?" chirped Mike coming into the room. "You look funny. Are you sick?"

"Oh, nothing, nothing. Just some gas," said Peter, rising and quickly stuffing the letter into his pocket. He didn't want Mike to read about his father just yet in case it didn't work out.

"So, is everything at home OK?"

"Yes, yes. Going along. They are eager to have us return, that's for sure."

The second letter only had his name and room number on the outside. The clerk said it had been received by a delivery service that afternoon. He opened it up. The stationary surprisingly carried The European Union official logo at the top.

Dear Peter,

The Authorities have allowed me to write this letter to you. I want to sincerely thank you for your friendship. I wasn't deserving of it as I lied to you about the money. Sorry, it had nothing to do with aid for refugees, just a good cover. I was indeed a paid courier for illegal drug businesses and I will suffer for my actions.

The authorities were following a money laundry trail and they had an informant on board the Majestic who tracked me. You showed me such honesty that it shamed me into confessing my part when questioned. Of course, you are innocent of any involvement. Fortunately, I have been given some leniency for my willing cooperation with the ongoing investigation.

I know it's a poor excuse, but I was tempted about money, probably like Roger. I plan to be very different in the future. I'll always remember your fine example. Thank you again. My best to Michael and his future.

Emma.

P.S. The confiscated money will be used as evidence but I'm told that it will be then donated to the UN Relief Fund for Refugees in the Balkans.

Deception was a hard pill to swallow for Peter and the surprise information from Emma really disturbed him. He wondered who was the informant, the spy. Possibly Roger? But if he were a government agent, his stealing the money didn't make much sense. Anyone else? In his mind he scanned the passengers but didn't find an answer.

However, Emma's mystery was solved and he hoped her world could rectify itself someday. He was glad that his own entangled connection suddenly was clearer even though he felt like a fool. He folded the letter and slowly replaced it in the envelope, giving it to Mike to read. The youngster was inquisitive and should know about it.

As Mike read, his face showed shock. "Gee, Gramps, this is so…so …"

"Surprising? Yes, Mike, I know what you mean. The world is full of unknowns, my boy. They can be both good and bad, be it past, present or future." Even his dear mother had hidden known facts but her secret was out of deep concern. Emma's greed and deception had, however, put them in harm's way.

"I thought she was nice. I'm disappointed," said Mike.

"So am I. But we've learned a lesson, I think. Not to be so gullible."

"But she said she was sorry, that's something."

"I hope she was sincere. Many people are sorry when they get caught, Mike, I hate to say. Not for what they did before but for what will come afterwards for them," said Peter, grudgingly.

Mike struggled to find an answer. "But the end seemed pretty good, didn't it? The money is going to a good cause." The grandson was still trying hard to be optimistic. "And she said you helped her, in a good way."

"Well, we'll have to leave it at that, Mike, but thanks. We have to be forgiving in our thoughts." Then turning to his grandson, Peter said, almost in tears, "I hope this didn't spoil anything for you. I wanted you to have good memories about our trip."

"For sure, Gramps. I had loads of fun with you and I got to know Kari. And I saw great stuff in Europe that I'll never forget. Not ever, ever."

"That's good," he said to Mike, hugging him. "Now it's time that we're going home. Got things to do,"

"Yep, I do agree. But I'll sure miss the food here." They both smiled.

The next day on the plane, Mike was fittingly on his last

sketch book page and he drew the Danube below them with barges and cruise ships on the sparkling water, churches and castles along the banks. He was saying goodbye to his journey of discovery with landmarks, cities and people. But for Peter, the farewell was also one of understanding, acceptance and reconciliation, just like Margie had predicted.

It was indeed a journey of love, deep and dear.

Also by Shirley D. Meier

Historical Fiction - **The Tangled Trail** (Outskirts Press, Colorado Independent Publishers Assoc.)

Travel non-fiction - **Four Points in Time and Place** (Outskirts Press)

Biography - **Ann Fort, Threads of a Splendid Life** (Outskirts Press)

Genealogy (co-author) - **Ding-Dind Familienchronik** (HVA Graishe Betriebe, Germany)

Memoir - **Stierum** (Journal, American Historical Society of Germans from Russia)

> **Prairie Patterns** (Journal, American Historical Society of Germans from Russia)

> **Holiday Memories** (North West Suburban Herald, Chicago)

Poetry - **Legacy of 1983 Glen Ullin, ND Centennial** (Bismarck Tribune))

> **Mood of a Mexican Town** (Triton IL College Salute to the Arts, The National Poetry Anthology.)

Drama - **Deborah**, one act. (produced by Hoffman Estates IL High School)

Short Story – **Out to Pasture** (South Glen Library Publication, Centennial, CO)

Essay (Educational) - **German as a Second Language in America.** (Babel, Australian Language Association Journal)

Dakota Deutsch (Journal, American Historical Society of Germans from Russia)

Writing across the Curriculum (Illinois Writer's Project)

More Balance is Needed in Educations' Balancing Act (Illinois Pioneer Press)

Illinois Goal Assessment Program (Journal, International Reading Association).

A Writing Project, Training Teachers of Composition from Kindergarten to College (Heinemann Educational Books)

Multi-Cultural Teaching – (Free Berlin University, Germany)

Literary collection - (co-author) - **Views...From Jack Ass Hill.** (Wasteland Press)

Anthology (editor) - **Directions** (Scholastic Press)

Yearbook (editor) – **The Halcyon** (Columbia Scholastic Press, Northern IL Press Assoc.

CPSIA information can be obtained
at www.ICGtesting.com
Printed in the USA
BVHW080750260821
615084BV00002B/114